# Geronimo Stilton

# THE BATTLE FOR CRYSTAL CASTLE

## THE THIRTEENTH ADVENTURE IN THE KINGDOM OF FANTASY

Scholastic Inc.

Published by Scholastic Inc., *Publishers since 1920*, 557 Broadway, New York, NY 10012. SCHOLASTIC and associated logos are trademarks and/or registered trademarks of Scholastic Inc.

*Stilton is the name of a famous English cheese. It is a registered trademark of the Stilton Cheese Makers' Association.*

Library of Congress Cataloging-in-Publication Data available

ISBN 978-1-338-65501-8

Text by Geronimo Stilton
Original title *L'impero della fantasia*
Cover by Danilo Barozzi
Art director Roberta Bianchi
Illustrations by Silvia Bigolin, Carla Bebernardi, Ivan Bigarella, Alessandro Muscillo, and Danilo Barozzi and Christian Aliprandi
Art direction by Lara Martinelli
Art assistant Andrea Alba Benelle
Graphics by Marta Lorini

Special thanks to Shannon Decker
Translated by Julia Heim
Interior design by Becky James

10 9 8 7 6 5 4 3 2 1                    20 21 22 23 24

Printed in China              62

First edition, September 2020

# MORE THAN A KINGDOM . . . AN EMPIRE!

**D**ear Rodent Friends, Long, looooong, loooooooong ago there was an enormouse mythical land:

*the legendary Empire of Fantasy!*

It was so big that it contained all of the different Kingdoms of Fantasy. No one was ever able to explore it all! It was so beautiful that to understand its MAGNIFICENCE you had to let your imagination take over . . .

But soon an evil wizard took control, turning those splendid valleys into gray and desolate lands. Only the Kingdom of Fantasy survived the attack.

Then, one day, a band of heroes decided to set off on an epic journey to bring the great empire back to life. I can't wait to tell you their story — it will make your heart pound!

That's the truth, or my name isn't *Geronimo Stilton*!

# FANTASTICAL STORIES

It was a crisp autumn evening in New Mouse City, perfect for resting after a long day, snacking on a cheesy treat, and maybe even popping your snout into a good **B**|**O**|**O**|**K**!

And that was exactly what I was going to do. Though, to be honest, the book was popping out at me! See, I was reading a pop-up book. How fabumouse!

At *The Rodent's Gazette*, we had decided to create a new line of pop-up books, Fantastical Stories, to spark readers' imaginations! Oh, wait, I forgot to introduce myself . . .

My name is Stilton, *Geronimo Stilton*, and I run *The Rodent's Gazette*, the most famous newspaper on Mouse Island!

As I was saying, I had to make sure that every page of the *Fantastical Stories* pop-up book was perfect, because it was going to print the next day! I didn't want to disappoint my nephew Benjamin — he adores FANTASY books.

How marvelmouse!

I knew it would make Benjamin happy to read about the adventures of wizards, fairies, and enchanted castles on those colorful pages. But I also wanted to impress Grandfather William. Otherwise, he would have put me in those pages, too . . . as a BOOKMARK! *Squeak!* →

As I looked through the illustrations, I calmed down. Everything was going to be okay, I could feel it! The stories were truly fascinating, and the art was so fabumouse that I felt like I was living the adventures. I opened to the first story, "The Dragon with the Golden Crest." I felt like I was flying with the dragon!

Then I read the story

of "The Thousand-Year-Old Dragon." I felt like I had landed inside a fairy-tale castle, full of secret passageways and enchanted rooms that sparkled with magic!

Then I flipped to the first page of another adventure: "The Rebel Princess." There was something very strange in those illustrations, something magical but familiar. I bent over to get a better look at the book. My snout got closer to the page . . . and a little closer . . . and a little closer still . . . until a spark blinded me, and a sudden gust of hot air surrounded me.

Before I knew what was happening,

I was falling into the pages!

# A Familiar Castle

For a brief moment I felt like I was flying. Then I landed with a thud and looked around, confused.

I was in a forest with trees whose branches swayed in the wind. The sky was a crystal blue. In the distance, I saw a magnificent palace.

Holey cheese — that was the castle that I had been looking at in the *Fantastical Stories* book! Had I ended up inside the book? How was that even possible? I mean, I love getting into stories, but not like this!

I gathered my courage and decided to walk toward the palace. There had to be someone there who could help me!

I WALKED AND WALKED AND WALKED until I was tired, exhausted, completely and totally spent!

Finally, I got up close and saw the sparkling blue castle. I rubbed my eyes. Could it really be? This looked like **Crystal Castle**, where Blossom, the Queen of the Fairies of the Kingdom of Fantasy, lived. If it was, my friend would definitely be able to help me! I ran even faster to the front gate. When I arrived at the castle, my heart was pounding . . .

# A MYSTERIOUS
# GREETING

When I opened the door, it really hit me that Crystal Castle wasn't an illustration in the pages of a book anymore — it was real and as beautiful as only **Blossom's** palace could be!

How exciting! I had returned to the most incredible world that ever existed: the Kingdom of Fantasy! I'd had so many adventures here already. Who knew how many more awaited me.

I wandered around the castle, searching for my friend, until I found myself in a hall at the very top. An unmistakable *smell* filled my snout: the delicate rose scent that surrounded Blossom wherever she went! I looked around . . . but there was no one there.

How strange! Blossom usually greeted me

warmly when I arrived at Crystal Castle. Suddenly, a voice echoed through the room:

"Knight . . . ight . . . ight!"

Who said that?! The room was empty, and I could hear the voice echo!

"Knight . . . ight . . . ight!"

There it was again! But where was the voice coming from? At that moment, a figure crossed the room as fast and light as a breeze. It was wearing a long tunic and had a hood over its head. It turned, and in a flash I saw a lovely face: Blossom!

"My Queen!" I exclaimed.

I rushed over to her, but in my hurry I stumbled over

my paws and nearly TUMBLED snout over tail! Blossom's laughter rang through the air so joyfully that it sounded like tinkling bells. Then she disappeared, vanishing through the other side of a door . . . and leaving me stunned in the middle of the hall.

How strange! That wasn't something Blossom would do! Why had she run away? And why was she wearing that **dark cloak**?

Before long, that unmistakable rose scent filled my snout again . . . and there was Blossom!

"Knight, I am so happy to see you at the castle again. It's been too long!" she said.

My Queen!

I bowed politely and said, confused, "I'm also happy to see you, My Queen! But

didn't we just see each other just a moment ago?"

Blossom wrinkled her forehead. "No, Knight! I just got here."

"But then who was that before?" I squeaked.

Blossom seemed just as confused as me. "Before? What do you mean?"

"You . . . she . . . the face . . . the voice . . . even the rose scent . . ." I stammered.

The queen gave me a smile that lit up the room. "Knight, perhaps you're a bit tired from your trip! Unfortunately, there isn't much time to rest."

Blossom stopped smiling, as if a cloud had come over her. "I have some **BAD** news. The Kingdom of Fantasy is in trouble. That is why I called you here, my brave friend: We need your help!"

My whiskers sagged. I did not like to see Blossom so upset. What threat was she talking about?

I quickly reassured her. "Tell me what I can do,

and I will do it!"

She gestured to me and said,

"Follow me, and you can see for yourself."

# THE MISSING TREASURE

I followed Blossom through the mazelike halls of Crystal Castle. My whiskers were trembling with worry. The trip seemed really

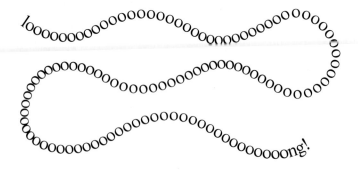

loooooooooooooooooooooooooooooooooooooooooooooooooooooooooooooooooooooooooooooooooooooooooooooooooooooooong!

We finally arrived outside a room shaped like a circle. I realized that it had to contain something super important, because it was surrounded by many **GUARDS**.

And what strange guards they were! They all

had an odd look about them. Some had **HUGE EYES** as big as soccer balls, others had **giant ears** as big as sails, and the rest of them had TREMENDOUS NOSES as big as hills!

They see all . . .

Blossom turned to look at me. "Knight, let me introduce the vigilant *Watchful Guardians*, the most dependable watchmen in the Kingdom of Fantasy. Nothing has ever escaped their gaze, their hearing, or their smell!" Then the queen sighed. "Unfortunately, even they were not able to protect what was **HELD** in this room. That's how all this started!"

They hear all . . .

They smell all.

**WHAT?**

19

Someone had gotten past these guards without being seen, heard, or smelled? Holey cheese, **how was that possible**?

When we entered the round room, I was stunned. It was full of strange characters waving magnifying glasses, measuring tools, and other things. They looked like they were trying to find the answer to an impossible problem.

Looking more closely, I realized that many of

them were examining the area all around a big crystal case, on a crystal pedestal, shaped like a flower made of crystal!

Inside the **CASE**, there was a satin pillow that looked so soft that it made me want to curl up and take a nap — but there was nothing on it!

Something very important was missing, a treasure that the Watchful Guardians weren't able to protect.

Finally, Blossom spoke up. "Knight, now you can see why I am so worried. That glass case used to hold the **Harmony Stone** . . . but it was stolen!"

"Holey cheese," I said in shock. "It was really precious, right?"

Blossom nodded. "It's an ancient stone from the earliest times of the Kingdom of Fantasy. It symbolizes the strength of the kingdom. Without it, the kingdom is weaker!"

Just then, a man with a mustache so long it brushed the ground came running over to meet us. He was jotting things down in a small notebook and shouting, "My Queen, ze zituation iz zerious! My collaboratorz are trying to dizcover where the thief disappeared to, but it'z impozzible to understand! Haz the brave, couragiouz, fearlezz helper you were expecting arrived yet?"

Ze zituation is zerious!

As soon as he saw me, the man seized a thick magnifying glass from his pocket. He looked me up and down, from the ends of my ears to the tip of my tail.

"Zis iz him?" he asked, a bit disappointed.

I cleared my throat. "Um, my name is Stilton, *Geronimo Stilton*, and I am not brave,

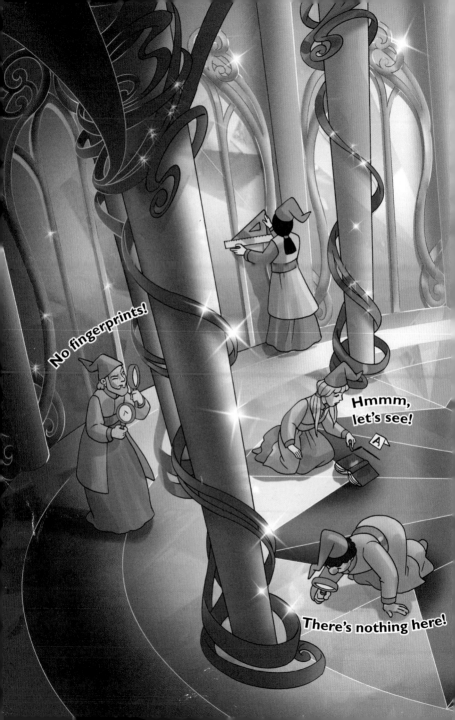

courageous, or fearless! To tell you the truth, I'm a total 'fraidy mouse!"

Blossom corrected me. "My friend is very modest. He doesn't know his own strength! This is the valiant and fearless **Knight** I told you about!"

The man's face broke into a huge smile, and his mustache curled upward.

"You should have zaid that at onze!" he cried. "Let me introduze myself: I'm Profezzor Barnaby Grumbledon, Expert in Ztrange Phenomena, Dizappearancez, Abzurd Epizodes, and the Unexplainable!"

He shook my paw very hard, and his smile made his cheeks grow as round as two balls of mozzarella. Had I understood? He was a **detective** for the Kingdom of Fantasy?

"The pleasure's all mine," I said. "I would be happy to help you!"

**Professor Grumbledon's** mustache drooped, like two overcooked spaghetti noodles.

"I hope you can help, my friend," he said seriously. "Whoever ztole that preciouz ztone iz a very dangerouz thief!"

Blossom nodded. "That's why I called my trusted knight. We know now that the group that st°le the Harmony Stone is the most dangerous enemy the Kingdom of Fantasy has ever had . . .

THE INVISIBILE ARMY!"

# THE LEGEND OF
# THE EMPIRE

The Invisible Army? I had never heard of them, but my whiskers immediately *trembled* in fright!

Blossom continued, "The Invisible Army is our ancient enemy. Now that they have taken the Harmony Stone, we are weak and in serious danger. So the time has come: The ancient

## Legend of the Empire
## of Fantasy

is about to begin!"

I repeated, shaking my snout, "The Legend of the *Empire of Fantasy*?"

I've visited many places that are the stuff of legends: fascinating, scary, magical, enchanted, mysterious, incredible, mythical, terrifying, witchy, dragony, ogrey, trolly, elfin, princely, and knightly. But all of them had to do with the *Kingdom* of Fantasy — not the *Empire*!

Professor Grumbledon pointed his magnifying glass at my snout again. His mustache became as straight as two exclamation points. After an intense examination, he exclaimed, "I'm noting some confuzion on your face!"

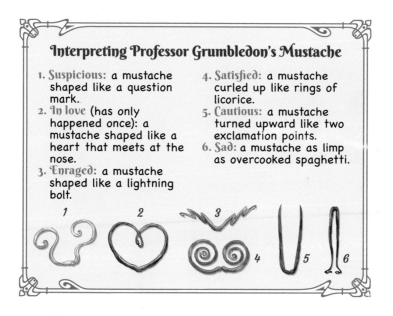

## Interpreting Professor Grumbledon's Mustache

1. **Suspicious:** a mustache shaped like a question mark.
2. **In love** (has only happened once): a mustache shaped like a heart that meets at the nose.
3. **Enraged:** a mustache shaped like a lightning bolt.
4. **Satisfied:** a mustache curled up like rings of licorice.
5. **Cautious:** a mustache turned upward like two exclamation points.
6. **Sad:** a mustache as limp as overcooked spaghetti.

Blossom nodded seriously and said, "I hoped that this moment would never come, my Knight, but it is time that you learn the story of the Kingdom of Blossom Valley and the Kingdom of Swamp Valley. Come with me to the **Legend Room**!"

The queen and Grumbledon led me to the library of enchanted books. There, we went down a spiral staircase hidden between the shelves and found ourselves in an enormouse underground room.

The walls were decorated with CRYSTAL tiles that had scenes from encounters with monsters and mythical creatures chiseled in. There were witches who captured princesses, damsels transformed into trees, unicorns, sirens, and even a lion with a serpent's tail spitting fire!

"All of the **LEGENDS**, myths, beliefs,

and prophecies that have ever existed in our world are etched here," Blossom explained.

As she said those words, she pushed aside a heavy velvet curtain to show me a hidden space. Holey cheese!

Inside, there was the largest book I had ever seen! It was so big that the cover touched the ceiling and you needed to climb a SUPER-TALL ladder to open it. All the books in my whole library couldn't add up to the number of pages in this one book!

Grumbledon said, "Here iz *The Book of All the Fantastical Legends* (including the terrible, dizazterous, tragic onez). There are 8,004,567, 844,322,670,500,000,362,109,080,045,678, 443,226,724,905,000,003,621,090 pages." He gestured to the ladder. "Please, climb up! You need to open the book to page 345,000,000,896,030."

I turned as pale as a ball of mozzarella!

"Don't worry," Grumbledon said. "I put a bookmark there!"

Grumbledon pointed to the ladder, and my mouth dried up!

"Me?" I squeaked. "Climb

How terrifying!

up there? I can't! I'm afraid of heights!"

But, when I saw the hopeful look on Blossom's face, I knew that there was no turning back.

I sighed. "Okay, up I go!"

I climbed slowly (very slowly) up the ladder, careful not to look down. Then I opened up the book to the page with the bookmark . . .

*and began to read.*

It is said that one day, long ago, there existed a place that is now unknown. At the Kingdom of Fantasy's distant border, people lived in joy, happiness, and order.

# The Legend of the Empire of Fantasy

*T*his was the Kingdom of Blossom Valley.
It exploded with flowers and all the strength its people could rally.
The people thrived peacefully and in harmony, and joined the other kingdoms to form the Empire of Fantasy!

Defending the empire was his aim,
from the rise of the sun,
until down it came.
Without brutal wars or cruelty,
just with true strength and beauty!
His armor, so colorful and festive,
had gone through the ages uncontested.
Whenever he started a tickle-toss fight,
he'd cause an excess of laughter and delight.

Then there was he who,
with a great sense of grace,
would shoot arrows to put kindness in place.
And if he struck an enemy with a heart so cruel,
the heart would be sweet as honey the moment he fell.

*D*on't forget the one who hit all that caused trouble
with a catapult full of relaxing bubbles!
Because those who are stressed can act out in crime,
it's always better to feel good and have a pleasant time!

*H*owever, it's certain that when goodness is spread,
there's always someone trying to tear it to shreds.
And so an evil and arrogant wizard
arrived with bad intentions as strong as a blizzard.
Quick as a whip he took all the power
and transformed the valleys into something much more dour.

*T*his wizard demolished
    and destroyed without
stopping.
  Even the beautiful
  rainbows started
  dropping!
    Slowly but surely,
    Blossom Valley became
    an ugly gray swamp
    that no one could tame.
    Its poor inhabitants,
    depressed and defeated,
    couldn't retaliate, and
    so they retreated.
    Everything they loved
    had suddenly vanished,
    so joy and delight had
    also been banished.

*T*he Kingdom of Blossom
   Valley disappeared and
became
the Kingdom of Swamp
Valley — it was never the
same.
It stunk, it was dark and
tremendously sad,
a place where nothing was
good and everything was bad.

*E*ven the army was fully
   transformed!
It became a gang of beasts to
   which no one warmed.

*T*he tickle-tosser developed
   a terrible flaw.
It became the dark whine-
tosser, and did not help at all.
It transformed all those hit
into great giant whiners,
a bunch of dull grumps to
which nothing was finer.

*M*uch the same thing happened with the arrows of kindness. They turned all that they hit into evil and blindness. These horrible, terrible arrows of aggression spread rage and bad attitudes in quick succession.

*A*nd those soft, sweet bubbles of relaxing prevention became only bubbles of stress and of tension. And thus all the hearts, deprived of all color, became filled with boredom and squalor.

$E$veryone turned more
and more gray
until they just vanished
in their dismay.
The wizard then placed a
horrible spell
ensuring that as Invisibles
they would dwell.
The Invisibles rebelled
against the empire
and broke it to bits,
fighting with fire.
Only the lone Kingdom of
Fantasy
resisted the attack and
sent them away.
But one day they may
return, in a scene truly
dire,
to attack what is left of
the empire!

# Blossom Valley

# Swamp Valley

# THE ISLAND OF THE SEVEN SECRETS

When I finished reading, I had chills down to my tail!

"And that day has arrived?" I asked, my whiskers quivering.

Grumbledon nodded. "Thatz right, Knight!"

Cheesy creampuffs! I imagined that the invisible soldiers were already there, ready to attack . . .

**what a feline fright!**

"How can we possibly save the kingdom from such a powerful enemy?" I asked.

Blossom smiled. "There is still a glimmer of hope, Knight. You haven't read the last part of the legend!"

Oops, silly me!

I turned the page and continued reading . . .

*F*or salvation, you'll need
   to locate the crown,
but to do that, true
wisdom must be
found.
With that object, the
empire can reunite
and defeat those who
seek to destroy and to
fight!
The Island of the Seven Secrets is
where it hides,
that rugged land with its steep walls
and sides.
The difficult path must be
crossed right;
the Mask of the Winged
Ones can bring it to
light.
Within the fifth day,
you must arrive . . .
If time runs out, you won't
escape alive!

I breathed a sigh of relief. We still had a chance!

"Stealing the stone is the first sign that the Invisibles want to **attack** us," Blossom said. "Only they could have made it past the Watchful Guardians — they have no color, no shape, and make no sound when they move!"

Rats, how terrifying! Just hearing Blossom talk about the Invisibles made my fur stand on end!

The queen continued. "Our kingdom is in danger, and there is only one way to save it and ensure peace:

*We must bring back the Empire of Fantasy!*

My bravest Knight, you must help us get the crown. You leave today for the Island of the Seven Secrets!"

*Squeak!*

I gathered my courage and asked, "But will you

come with me to the Island of the Seven Secrets, My Queen? And, um . . . can I get down from this ladder now?"

"You will have company on your journey, but it will not be I who joins you, my dear Knight," Blossom said kindly. "It will be a **courageous** leader! Come down now."

As I climbed down the ladder, I asked myself who the courageous leader might be. Who could possibly be worthy of taking Queen Blossom's place on this mission?

When I reached the ground, Blossom explained, "I must stay here to defend Crystal Castle from the attacking Invisibles, but I know that the leader I have chosen will not disappoint me! She is a bit impulsive, but that's to be expected — she's not even eighteen years old yet." She smiled proudly. "I can't wait for you to see how big and brave my beloved Winglet has gotten!"

I was squeakless.

WiNglet, Blossom's daughter?

WiNglet, the adorable little kid I had saved from the grasp of Crowbar the Cruel and his wife, Blossom's wicked twin sister, Wither?

Winglet, the sweetest and most enchanting creature in all the Kingdom of Fantasy, so sweet that just watching her sleep in her crib made me tear up?

Winglet, with big eyes as blue as cornflowers, tiny hands, and a heart as tender as the softest cheese? She was almost **eighteen years old**?

# TIME FLIES!

I shook my snout in disbelief. "My Queen, the last time I saw Winglet, she was a little child! How can she have grown up so fast?"

Blossom pointed to a pendulum clock in a corner of the room. "Remember that, in the Kingdom of Fantasy, **time** passes differently than it does in your world!"

Blossom was correct, of course. In the Kingdom of Fantasy, time could move as

SLOWLY

as a sleepy snail . . .

. . . Or time could pass as

QUICKLY as a racing rabbit!

Blossom placed some beautiful clothes into my paws. "Here is a uniform that is worthy of your long mission."

Long? Well, the legend did say five days, but thanks to the rules of time in the Kingdom of Fantasy, only a few moments would have passed in New Mouse City. I wouldn't even be late to hand in *Fantastical Stories* pages!

Suddenly, a powerful roar interrupted my thoughts.

# ROOOOAAAAR!!

Chattering cheddar — help!

A second later, a giant, terrifying white tiger leaped into the room!

It was light on its paws, and through my fear, I noticed that a young fairy was riding on its back. That was the same fairy I had mistaken for Blossom when I arrived!

"Hello, everyone!" she cried.

I was so shocked I couldn't even squeak. She was so different from any fairy I had ever seen in the Kingdom of Fantasy! She had *curly* hair that looked like it had been brushed by a tornado. Her face was as delicate as a butterfly's wings, her skin was a light blue, and her eyes were big and sparkling.

She was different from Blossom but *resembled* her a lot. When I finally recognized her, I felt myself melt like cheese left out in the hot sun.

Blossom scolded her kindly, "Winglet, dear, you know that I don't want Dawn running around inside Crystal Castle!"

*Winglet* jumped off the tiger's back and exclaimed, "But Mom, Dawn is just a cub!"

Then she turned toward me and said, "Finally

Hello, everyone!

we meet, fearless knight! I have heard many stories about you. You saved me when I was a **baby**!"

She threw her arms around my neck, and my fur turned bright red with embarrassment.

I cleared my throat. "Oh, I only did my duty,

Princess! But look at you! How you've grown!"

Blossom beamed. "Yes, Winglet is my pride and joy!"

She looked at Winglet with warm eyes. Too bad that the eyes watching me were cold and hungry . . . *squeak*! They belonged to Dawn the tiger, and she was staring at me like a tasty meal! Have I mentioned that cats make my whiskers tremble in fright?

Winglet noticed, and said, "Don't be scared of Dawn! She likes you a lot, I can tell by the way she's looking at you. You should pet her, or she might get offended!"

Sure, maybe she liked me . . . as a snack!

I reached out my paw verrrrry carefully and whispered, "Here, little tiger. Let me PET you!"

Suddenly, Dawn lay down with her belly in the air and started to purr so loudly that I could feel the ground shake under my paws!

Professor Grumbledon explained, "The princezz never zeparatez from her beloved white tiger." Then he added, under his breath, "And it's uselezz to try to give her rulez — she always doez thingz her own way. That'z why they call her the Rebel Princezz!"

Squeak!

# Winglet

**Who:** Blossom's daughter. Strong and impulsive, everyone calls her the Rebel Princess!

**Personality:** Fierce and courageous, she has a pure spirit and a big heart. She would do anything to defend the weak.

**Her passion:** She loves chess, drawing, and using a bow and arrow, which she is quite good at!

"I can hear you, you know!" Winglet piped up. "Yes, everyone calls me the Rebel Princess . . . and I like it that way!"

Blossom gave a cool smile. "My Winglet has so much energy. Luckily, she has a calm and poised young woman at her side: Flamelet."

Winglet took my paw and said quickly, "I can't wait to introduce you to her, Knight! I've only known her for a short time, but she's already my best friend! She is the one who gave me this!"

She pointed to the dragonfly-shaped barrette in her hair.

Winglet disappeared from the room faster than a mouse with a cat on its tail and returned a moment later holding the hand of a fairy with a wide, contagious smile. Even her hair looked happy — a sca of soft and wispy curls fell down her shoulders like a waterfall of rubies!

She greeted me with a deep bow and said, "I

# Flamelet

**Who:** A young woman who recently moved to Crystal Castle. She immediately became friends with Winglet, as if they'd always known each other.

**Personality:** She's an idealist like the princess, but is more mild-mannered and sweet. Her open smile and sincere eyes immediately made Winglet like her.

**Her passion:** She is great at drawing, but she can also bake tasty treats.

have heard so much about you, Knight! You are Winglet's hero!"

I blushed with **embarrassment**.

"Don't be fooled by her sweet and delicate air!" Winglet said to me. "*Flamelet* is a force of nature, especially when it comes to drawing! Do you want to see our work? Follow me!"

Without waiting for an answer, she dragged us outside, all the way to Crystal Castle's gardens.

Holey cheese! With Winglet along, the journey to the ISLAND OF THE SEVEN SECRETS would never be boring!

# PERFECT AIM

Winglet led us toward a magnificent garden overflowing with luxurious plants, trees, and flowers.

"Knight, this is my special place. Everyone calls it the Princess Garden!" she said proudly. "This is where I love to spend my time."

I peered around, amazed. Inside a gazebo was a table with a chessboard, and farther down were swords and spades of all shapes and sizes.

Throughout the garden there were **targets** so full of arrows that they looked like cacti. Winglet was quite the shot!

Finally, in the shadow of a great WILLOW TREE were two easels, each with a canvas and paintbrushes. Both canvases showed the same

subject, and both had the title *Lorian.*

"See?" Winglet showed us. "The first portrait was painted by Flamelet, and I did the second one."

Both paintings showed a **SERIOUS-LOOKING** young man. Flamelet's was lifelike and masterful. Winglet's was a funny CARICATURE with thick eyebrows and a frown that looked like it belonged to a troll in a bad mood.

Winglet giggled. "I think mine is closer to the original!"

Blossom sighed. "Winglet, you must stop making fun of Lorian! He is very brave and polite, and most importantly, he would do anything to **protect you**."

"That's the point," Winglet protested. "I don't need to be protected by anyone, least of all a pouting dragon tamer. He's a stuck-up know-it-all! I can take care of myself — and if I need help, I have Dawn!"

Cheese and crackers, Winglet really had an

**attitude**! Now I could see why they called her the Rebel Princess!

Winglet stormed off, and in the process, hit her foot against the rack that held the weapons. A heavy, long spear wobbled and fell from above. Just as it was about to fall on the princess . . .

**ZWIIP!!!**

An arrow shot into the column right between the spear and Winglet, blocking its fall! I squeaked, "Moldy mozzarella, what aim!"

The princess was saved!

*Careful, Princess!*

(No thanks to me.) I turned to see a young man with a bow in his hand. He was the one who shot the **>-arrow→** !

"Princess Winglet," he said seriously, "you aren't lacking in talent, but your weak spot is your recklessness!"

Yikes!

Blossom and Flamelet darted to Winglet to make sure that she was okay, then Blossom turned to the young man. "**LORIAN!** I cannot thank you enough for everything you do."

Looking at me, she added, "Knight, Lorian is a valiant dragon tamer who has protected Winglet

# LORIAN

**Who:** Raised by a family of dragon tamers with ancient origins, his job is to protect Princess Winglet.

**Personality:** He is determined and sure of himself, and has only one objective: to be worthy of the duty that the queen has given him.

**His passions:** He is quite skilled in martial arts, with a bow and arrow, and in the noblest knightly subjects! He is also accompanied by a loyal Emerald Dragon.

since she was a child! He will join you on your journey. I'm sure he will be an incredible help."

Lorian introduced himself with a bow and a deep voice. "Pleased to meet you, Knight."

I bowed back and said, "Surely Winglet and I will be happy to —"

But Winglet interrupted. "Mom, I already told you that I'm not going on that trip! I will stay here and **defend** Crystal Castle with you!"

Blossom shook her head. "Your mission is extremely important. Stopping the Invisible Army will be pointless if we do not form a new empire founded on **good**. You are the only one with the strength, the courage, and the determination to find the ancient **Crown of the Empire**."

At that moment, two guards darted into the garden, breathless. "Your Majesty! The Invisible Army is at the doors, ready to attack!"

# THE ALLIANCE OF THE WINGED ONES

O ur worst nightmares were coming true!

We ran to high ground in front of the castle, where we could see the border of the Kingdom of Fairies. Blossom stared at the **horizon** through a crystal telescope and let out a worried sigh.

"They are closer than I thought," she said. "See for yourself!"

She handed me the telescope, and I began to tremble in fright. In the distance, a giant cloud of dust headed toward the castle. I couldn't see warriors, horses, or helmets or armor, just the tips of spears and studded clubs, ready to attack. Meanwhile, a horrific stench had begun spreading through the air!

I gulped. "My Queen, how will we fight against

such fierce, stinky, and **invisible** enemies?"

Blossom frowned. "It will be the terrible stench of the Invisibles that will help us in battle. It's the only way we will sense where they are. The **Alliance of the Winged Ones** will defend us! We have asked the thirteen kingdoms that are faithful to the fairies to create a union that will fight together against the enemy."

"To win, we muzt overcome all our differencez and fight az one!" Grumbledon added.

Two more guards darted up to

### The Winged Ones

The Winged Ones are an ancient dynasty of creatures with the purest and most sincere of hearts. They are able to provoke immense love in all living creatures. They have blue skin like the sky, and light and transparent wings like their hearts.

Blossom. "The **Winged Ones** have arrived at Crystal Castle. They are waiting for you in the Meeting Room!"

We followed Blossom back into the palace. I was surprised and thrilled to see some creatures from the Kingdom of Fantasy that I was already very good *friends* with:

▣ *Sterling,* the Princess of the Silver Dragons (and just as proud as I remembered!);

▣ *Firebreath III,* the leader of the Fire Dragons (I didn't remember his fangs looking quite so sharp!);

▣ *King Thunderhorn* and his elves;

▣ the blue unicorns, led by *King Skywings;*

▣ *Firebeard* and the Red-nosed Gnomes (with their unmistakable apple-shaped hair);

▣ *King Longlegs the Thirteenth* and the Invisible Spiders;

▣ *Sweet Melinda* and the Vanilla Fairies;

🔲 the Blue Weasels led by *Wink*;

🔲 the *Crystalline Gnomes*;

🔲 *Giant Strongheart*;

🔲 *Aquafin's* mermaids;

🔲 *King Chuckles's* Pixies;

🔲 and, finally, *Queen Chocolatina's* Gingerbread men!

They were all ready for battle, ready to defend the Kingdom of Fantasy!

I was touched by their courage. They all yelled at once, lifting their spears, shields, bows and arrows, and even the baskets of apples that the Red-nosed Gnomes were planning to use for the catapults.

"For the Alliance of the Winged Ones!"

"For the Alliance of the Winged Ones!" I yelled, joining them with my heart full of emotion.

GAME

A pixie has lost his hat!
Can you find it?

The answer is on
page 78.

"For the Alliance of the Winged Ones!" Winglet repeated, holding her bow PROUDLY, ready to lead the entire group.

The alliance didn't even have time to march out of the room before a loud uproar echoed through the castle.

The noise was coming from the main entrance to Crystal Castle. The Invisibles were tearing it to pieces!

Holey cheese, I was too fond of my fur!

The fairy soldiers guarding the castle dashed into the room. "The Invisibles have reached Crystal Castle! **THEY ARE ATTACKING!** Prepare a defense!"

* Answer to the game on page 76–77: The hat is at the bottom left of the image, near Dawn's paw.

I began to shake like cheesy pudding, but next to me, Queen Blossom stayed calm and strong. She was ready to face the enemy.

WHAT COURAGE!

At that moment, the door to the Meeting Room was broken down. The sound was deafening!

Then a thunderous voice called out,

"WHERE DO YOU THINK YOU'RE GOING?"

# THE INVISIBLES ATTACK!

Did you think the booming voice belonged to a furious, threatening, terrifying giant? I WISH! It was worse, much worse! Because when the voice thundered, no one entered the room, not even a fly!

I turned to Blossom. "Wh-who s-s-said that?"

"I did, rat!" the thundering voice replied. "Ha, ha, ha, ha, ha!"

Then, as if by magic, a super-ugly creature appeared in the middle of the room! His features were hard like rocks, and he had such cruel eyes, it seemed like they were shooting out lightning bolts.

## IT WAS AN INVISIBLE!

The air whirled around him, gray and faded like a storm cloud.

Just looking at him, my heart filled with terror!

Blossom turned to me. "That is the Invisibles' great power — they can appear and disappear at will, so their attack is always surprise!"

The Invisible thundered, "Well said, Queen! You have Cruelardo Glowerface's word, as General Leader of the Invisible Army: We have come to destroy you! Attack!"

In the shake of a whisker, a crowd of soldiers ran into the room.

They all appeared from nowhere, just like their leader!

The allied forces fought back as best as they could, but the Invisibles disappeared just as suddenly as they had appeared!

Their weapons whirled about in the air, releasing sparks and making loud clangs!

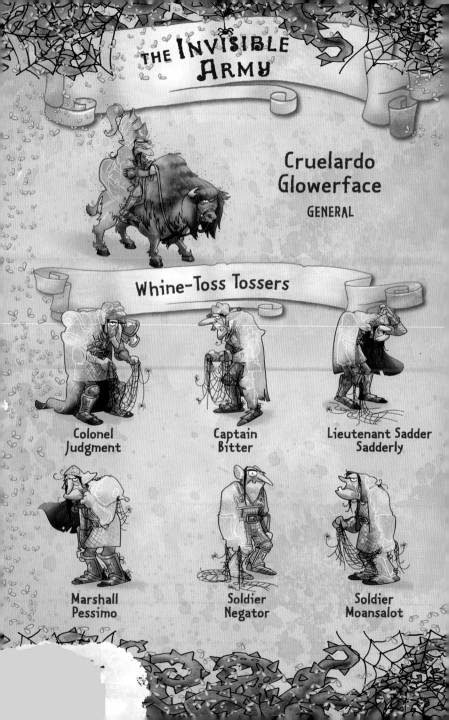

# THE INVISIBLE ARMY

## Cruelardo Glowerface
### GENERAL

## Whine-Toss Tossers

**Colonel Judgment**

**Captain Bitter**

**Lieutenant Sadder Sadderly**

**Marshall Pessimo**

**Soldier Negator**

**Soldier Moansalot**

# Shooters of the Arrows of Aggression

**Colonel Uglydud**

**Captain Scour**

**Lieutenant Destructo**

**Marshall Nasterly McNasty**

**Soldier Wicked Wrongwright**

**Soldier Longsword the Hideous**

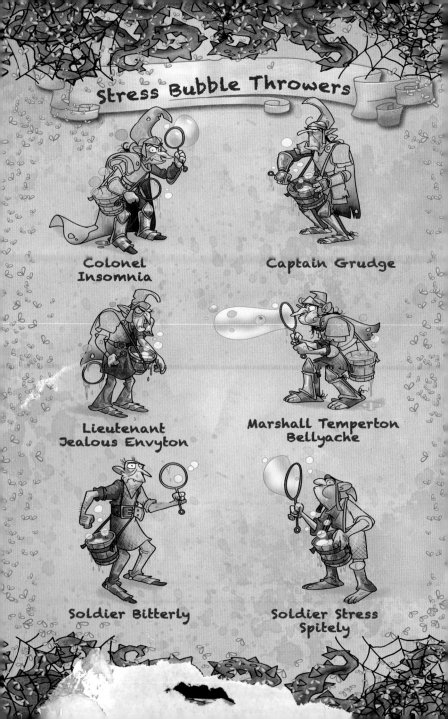

## I HAD NEVER SEEN SUCH A FIERCE BATTLE!

Winglet was about to launch an arrow, but Blossom stopped her. Then she grabbed me by the paw and said, "Quick! You, Winglet, and Lorian must leave for the ISLAND OF THE SEVEN SECRETS. If you don't find the crown, we'll never be able to SAVE the empire!"

"My Queen, I will make sure Winglet gets there safely — knight's honor!" I vowed.

"I trust you with all my heart," Blossom said. "Winglet has a thousand talents, but she can also be careless! I hope some of your wisdom rubs off on her."

The queen smiled, then pulled out a mask and handed it to Winglet.

"This is the MASK from the Legend of the Empire," she explained. "It will help you find the path. Go east. When you reach the borders of the Kingdom of Fantasy, put the mask on. It will give you clues to figure out where to go."

The Rebel Princess took the mask but protested fiercely. "Mom, I don't want to leave you here to fight for our kingdom all by yourself!"

Blossom was holding back tears.

*"my sweet daughter, please, trust me."*

Winglet and Blossom exchanged a meaningful glance, one that only a mother and daughter could share. Then they **hugged** each other tight.

Winglet sighed and said, "All right, Mom. I will return with the crown!"

# At the Border of the Kingdom

Escaping Crystal Castle was not easy! The Invisibles kept vanishing from under our noses and popping up behind us, swinging at us with clubs and rusty weapons. *Squeak!*

Luckily, Winglet and Lorian were incredibly courageous and skilled. They were able to keep the Invisibles away from us as we ran toward the castle door.

I turned one last time to look back at Blossom's army. I knew they would defend Crystal Castle bravely, but I could only hope that they would hold off the enemy until we returned.

We climbed onto Dawn's back and escaped. Even though I was still truly terrified, that tiger was fabumously fast!

Winglet was **sad** that she couldn't say good-bye to Flamelet, but in all the confusion, there was no sign of her friend.

As soon as we were outside the castle, Lorian whistled. I heard wings flapping overhead. I looked up to see that the sun had darkened, like in an eclipse. Then a powerful

**RRROOOOOOOAAAAARRRRRR**

filled the sky, and a giant dragon landed next to us! Holey cheese — compared to that dragon, Dawn's roar seemed like a tiny meow!

Lorian caressed the dragon, and he lowered his head in greeting. The dragon was covered in sparkly green scales that looked like a cloak made of gemstones.

Moldy mozzarella, this must be the Emerald

Dragon that was always by Lorian's side!

The dragon tamer turned to him with deep respect. "Thank you for coming, Narek. Please come with us to the border of the Kingdom of Fantasy!"

The dragon agreed and knelt so that Lorian and I could climb onto his back. I'd barely had time to grab hold of his scales when . . .

ZOOM! We darted upward like a rocket!

"Hang on tight!" Lorian warned me. He didn't have to tell me twice! Winglet and Dawn grew smaller and smaller below us.

I pointed to them and suggested, in a quivering voice, "Couldn't we run along with them? I didn't mention this before, but . . . I'm afraid of HEIGHTS!"

Lorian reassured me calmly, "If you should fall, Knight, there's no need to worry: Narek would catch you in midair!"

Holey cheese, I hoped I never had to test the skills of that dragon!

From above, we could see the DAMAGE that the Invisibles had left behind. The tall trees, the splendid flowers, and the bright green grass of the Kingdom of Fantasy had all been reduced to sludge! There was no doubt about it — the Invisibles wanted to turn what was left of the kingdom into a deserted and COLORLESS land. We couldn't let that happen!

Lorian spurred Narek to fly faster, and Dawn had no trouble keeping up. That tiger ran like LIGHTNING!

We sped on, the sun above our heads a constant reminder of the time passing.

We crossed valleys, fields, forests, and plains, and only after many hours did we see the air around us start to shimmer. We had made it to the BORDER OF THE KINGDOM OF FANTASY!

91

Winglet pointed to a place up ahead and announced, "We've arrived!"

I breathed a deep sigh, full of anxiety, fear, but also hope. This was where our journey to the Island of the Seven Secrets would really begin!

Journey to the
Island of the Seven Secrets

# SECRETS REVEALED

Just on the other side of the border of the Kingdom of Fantasy were endless possibilities . . . but we didn't have the slightest idea which **direction** to go!

Narek landed in a clearing next to Dawn. "Maybe we should use the MASK OF THE WINGED ONES," Winglet suggested. "It could give us a clue!"

The princess pulled out the mask and put it on. She looked in front of her,

up → and down,
above
↑ and ↓ below
to the left ↺ and ↻ to the right.

My heart pounded while I waited . . . but Winglet didn't say anything!

Instead, she climbed a nearby **tree** to see beyond the leaves, she studied the skyline, she even started turning over stones!

Finally, the disappointed princess said, "I don't see **anything** here. Nothing, not a single thing!"

She stood up and took off the mask with a deep sigh.

I don't see a thing!

This wasn't good! How would we find our way?

Lorian stood off to one

side. Suddenly, he cleared his throat. "Princess, allow me to suggest something: There are **SECRETS** that only reveal themselves to those who know how to look. Be patient! The magic of the mask will guide you. Take a deep breath, just like in our meditation excrcises at Crystal Castle. Remember?"

Winglet rolled her eyes. "How could I forget? They were so boring! Here goes Lorian again. You'll get used to this, Knight. I just hope he doesn't keep it up the whole trip!"

Oh no! It seemed like a **STORM** was coming — and its name was Winglet!

Lorian responded calmly, "You might use your energy more productively, instead of wasting it ranting about me. Don't you think that would be better for our mission?"

Annoyed, Winglet cried, "Did you eat a B O O K for breakfast?" Then she turned to me. "Oh, Knight! Do you hear how he talks?"

Lorian was definitely very serious, but I could also tell that he was very WISE.

Moldy mozzarella, what a mess!

Winglet kept grumbling, but eventually she put on the mask again and took a deep breath. After a moment, she said, "Hmm, I just don't see any —"

Then she gasped. "There! Down there! I see a sparkly golden trail! It's as if the mask is pointing to the path we need to take. Quick, let's go!"

We all followed Winglet. After a few steps, suddenly we could all see the GOLDEN PATH!

Lorian recited, *"The difficult path must be crossed right; the Mask of the Winged Ones can bring it to light.*

"We are on the path that the Legend of the Empire talked about," Lorian said. "And the mask showed it to Winglet."

"We already know that," she huffed impatiently. "Come on, let's go!"

But suddenly, she stopped. "Wait! I saw something else . . ."

She leaned over behind a BUSH, reaching for something that was still invisible to us. Suddenly, a key appeared in her hand. It was a very strange shape.

"What could that open?"
I asked, excited.

We all noticed that there
was a kind of decoration that
looked like a SPIDERWEB
on the top of the key.

Winglet looked up at Lorian
and grumbled, "I have to admit, sometimes you're
right. When I looked carefully, the mask showed
me the path and a clue!"

Lorian smiled, and I breathed a sigh of relief.
But there was no time to waste! We had to keep
going if we were going to figure out what that key
opened.

Winglet led the way to the long golden path,
up and up into the woods. The branches
around us became tangled and thick, and
eventually they created a ceiling!

There were thick SPIDERWEBS hanging from

the branches that looked like the curtains of a ghost theater! *Squeak!*

Suddenly, the golden path stopped and we could see something sparkle in the tangle of branches. It was a **LOCK**!

We looked at each other nervously as Winglet inserted the key. It turned with a *click*, and a **tiny door** opened.

# A Masterful Spider

Have I already told you that I don't like buzzing wasps, stinging scorpions, or hissing snakes? Well, **spiders** aren't really my thing, either! And based on all those spiderwebs, there was surely one nearby. Something told me that it was **BIG** and **HAIRY**!

Winglet slowly drew her bow. "Don't worry, I'm here to defend you!" But even though she tried to look confident, her hands were trembling.

We walked into an **ENORMOUSE** room. The floor, the walls, and the ceiling were all made of tree branches braided together. The whole space was decorated with woven **wall hangings** made of what looked like fine silk. They were truly amazing!

Whoever had made the tapestries must have been a great artist. There were portraits of people, landscapes, scenes from everyday life, spiders eating insec — What?! When I looked more closely, I noticed that all of the wall hangings showed . . .

spiders, spiders, and more spiders!

There were lady spiders in elegant dresses, in the landscapes you could see spiders walking in meadows, and there were even portraits of baby spiders! Then it dawned on me — all of the tapestries were woven from spiderwebs!

Before I could hightail it out of there, we heard some strange sounds at the back of the room, behind a strange curtain (made of spiderwebs, of course!).

Holey cheese, it seemed like they were *cutting* something!

Winglet pulled back the curtain.

A giant, super-hairy spider stared at us from above with GIGANTIC EYES.

I bet he was thinking, *How lucky! Today we change up the menu! Instead of the usual fly, I've caught a dragon, a tiger, a fairy, a knight, and a mouse in my web!* In one leg he was holding a NEEDLE and thread, and in another a pair of SCISSORS he was using to cut. That's what all that noise was — and that's who'd made those amazing wall hangings!

Suddenly, the spider's look became fiercer. I turned to see what he was peering at. *Squeak!* We had ruined one of his most precious wall hangings when we came in!

I scrambled to fix the BROKEN art as best I could, trying to retie the broken threads.

"There, done!" I said finally. "So sorry if we ruined your work, Mr. Spider!"

But the spider was even more furious when he saw what a mess I'd made!

His voice was chilling. "It's useless for you to try to fix it. The damage is done!

# YOU WILL PAY FOR THIS!"

Dawn began to growl at him, and Winglet stroked her head. "Good girl, Dawn . . ."

Then Winglet turned to the spider.

What a mess!

"We don't want to bother you, but we need to go through here to continue on our important **MISSION**. May we pass?"

The spider responded with a threatening *snip* of his scissors. "First of all, my name isn't Mr. Spider, it's **Monsieur Arach**, master weaver. I've studied in very well-known dusty attics and the best abandoned cellars! What makes you think that I would let a delicious snack like you pass me by? I'd much rather you end up like that poor cocooned creature down there . . ."

Princess Winglet reflected for a moment. Then she put on the **MASK OF THE WINGED ONES** and explained, "This is the symbol of our research. If we don't continue on our mission, a cruel army will **DESTROY** our world!"

After thinking for a long while, the spider declared, "I will give you one chance. If you can weave a wall hanging that I like, I will let you pass. Otherwise . . . **I will eat you**!"

Eek! Oh, this conversation was spinning along in a crazy direction!

The spider made himself comfortable on an armchair, to enjoy the view.

We had no choice. If we wanted to escape that monstrous creature, we needed to weave a MAGNIFICENT WALL HANGING!

I will give you one chance!

# THE PERFECT TAPESTRY

What a disaster! We had to come up with something — and fast!

Lorian tried to lift our spirits. "Winglet, you're an ARTIST! I am sure that you can weave something beautiful!"

"I can draw and paint, but I'm awful with a needle and thread!" Winglet said nervously. "Just think of all the times that I practiced with my bow and arrow instead of finishing my *sewing* class at Crystal Castle! Flamelet would have made an absolute masterpiece." She sniffed.

The spider, meanwhile, wiggled his many legs impatiently. "So? Are you planning on weaving this wall hanging or not? My webs have no limits, but my *patience* sure does!"

Then his eyes focused on me. Cheese and crackers, I didn't like that one bit!

"I will start with you, RAT!" he said. "You will surely be a tasty treat, just like a bite of mosquito mousse!"

As he said that, a string of sticky, slimy green SALIVA trickled out of his mouth.

Out of fright, I stepped backward . . .

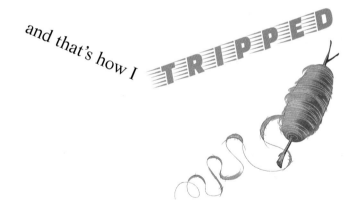

and that's how I TRIPPED

right on a **spool of webbing** that Monsieur Arach had left out for us to use!

In a flash, the thread got caught on my paw!

**Help!**

**Oops!**

I tried to free myself, but when I grabbed the webbing I got *tangled* even more!

I kept trying to rip the webbing off, and ended up even more knotted up . . . knotted knotted . . . knotted knotted . . . knotted . . . knotted . . . knotted . . .

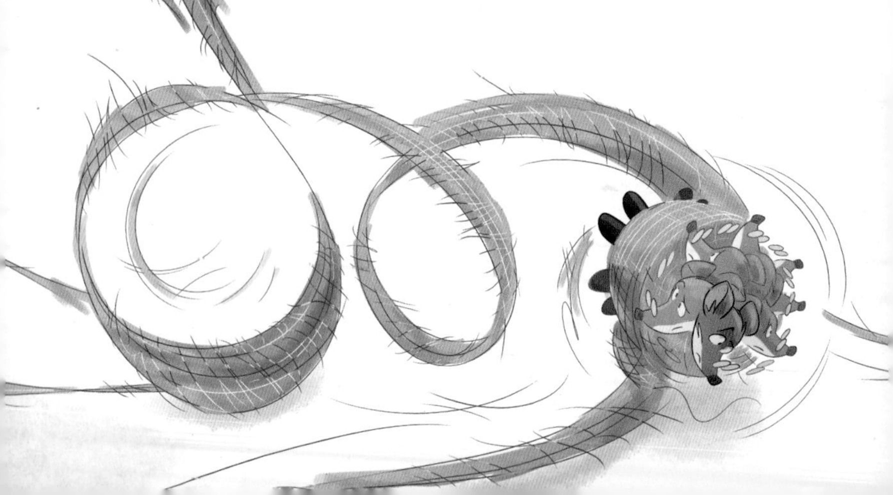

Suddenly, I tumbled to the ground like a heavy wheel of cheese and found myself completely tangled . . . tangled . . . tangled tangled . . . tangled . . . tangled

I don't know how, but I ended up snoutdown! I finally managed to free myself, lift myself with a jump, and . . .

Argh!

The **spider** got out of the armchair and stared at me hungrily.

I was prepared for the worst, when suddenly — he burst out **CRYING**!

Galloping Gouda! Was my work that **ugly**?

Then I heard sounds of admiration.

It was Winglet! "You are also an **extraordinary artist**!" she said.

I'm moved!

Between sobs, the spider said, "This . . . *sniff!* . . . is the most beautiful work I have ever seen! For a while now I have been looking for inspiration, a new creative push! I am so **moved**!"

Oh, for the love of cheese! Considering that I had been a spider snack minutes before, it seemed like everything was working out okay!

I blushed and replied, "Thank you. It was beginner's luck!"

Winglet spoke up. "Now we really must go!"

"Oh, of course!" said the spider, still absorbed in my work. "And thank you for this priceless masterpiece!"

The spider pulled one tapestry to the side, showing us a way out: THE GOLDEN PATH!

We were about to continue along the road when a stifled voice whispered, "Pssst! Where are you going? Don't leave me here, please! Free me!"

It was the **cocoon** hanging in the spider's lair.

Squeak, it was trying to get our attention!

"We can't leave a poor creature here!" Winglet said, ready to pull out her B°W and arrow.

"Poor creature?" the spider said. I could see that he was getting mad. "This little thief wanted steal all of my wall hangings in exchange for a bottle top! TAKE HER AWAY! It would be a great help to me."

I'll handle this!

Winglet didn't wait for him to say another word. She launched an **arrow**, which struck the thread that was keeping the creature hanging on the web. The bundle came down, and out popped — a fox!

"I'm finally free!" she shouted. Then she looked at Winglet with glittering eyes and added, "Wait,

I'm finally free!

you're Princess Winglet! What an honor to meet you. I'm **Foxlyn**! They call me the stingy fox, but I have no idea why. Do you happen to have some spare change, by any chance?"

Winglet smiled. "Where we're going, you don't need money. You just need heart and courage!"

I glanced over my shoulder. "Now let's hurry, before the spider changes his mind!"

Together, we headed down the golden path with our new friend!

# A Friend is . . .
## a Treasure?

The golden path continued upward through the tree branches, higher and higher and higher. The sun peeked from between the leaves, reminding us that we had very little **time** to find the island. We had no idea how much of our journey was left, and no idea how Blossom and the Winged Ones were doing!

Before I could lose myself in these thoughts, **Foxlyn's** chatter took over. "I heard you talking to the spider about your important mission and have some tools that I could sell you! A polish for dragon **SCALES**? A brush for knights' boots? Or perhaps an anti-flea medicine for Fluffy over here?"

# Foxlyn, the stingy fox

**Who:** The cleverest fox in all the kingdom.

**Personality:** She is long-winded and chatty, she has a great eye for business, and she's always looking to make some easy money. Where you see a worthless pebble, she sees a fashionable jewel. Where you see a piece of junk, she sees a priceless antique!

**Her passions:** Foxlyn would do anything to make a few dollars, even though she carries around a bag full of gold nuggets! Overall, it is said that she has a good heart and a generous spirit.

Foxlyn reached over to pet Dawn, but it wasn't a good idea — the tiger tried to **BITE** her paw!

"Her name is Dawn," Winglet said.

Foxlyn leaped back. "Maybe we'll save the anti-flea medicine for another time!" she said. "Well, if you change your mind, I'll give you my BUSINESS CARD."

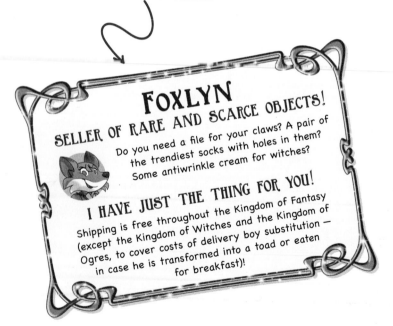

# FOXLYN
## SELLER OF RARE AND SCARCE OBJECTS!

Do you need a file for your claws? A pair of the trendiest socks with holes in them? Some antiwrinkle cream for witches?

## I HAVE JUST THE THING FOR YOU!

Shipping is free throughout the Kingdom of Fantasy (except the Kingdom of Witches and the Kingdom of Ogres, to cover costs of delivery boy substitution — in case he is transformed into a toad or eaten for breakfast)!

Winglet took the business card. After reading it, she said, "You must travel so much. You're so lucky! My dream is to explore the whole Kingdom of Fantasy. What places have you visited?"

The fox stroked the fur along her long, silky red tail. "Many, many places, Princess!

She grinned proudly. "Not to brag, but I have traveled far and wide in the Kingdom of Fantasy, and I have met many different creatures: fairies, dragons, gnomes, pixies, and **more**. I've been to the Land of Trolls, where I sold them violet soap; the Kingdom of the Fire Dragons, where I sold them ice pops; the Realm of the Towering Peaks, where I sold frozen foods; and the Kingdom of the Witches, where I sold beauty cream!"

Here you go, try it!

Holey cheese, she must have been a really great businessfox! Foxlyn had managed to sell **soap** to creatures who were completely against baths, and **ice pops** to creatures who hated ice! She sold **FROZEN FOODS** in the most

It freshens your breath!

whisker-freezing part of the Kingdom of Fantasy, and **beauty cream** to those who competed to see who was ugliest!

"But," Foxlyn added, "things haven't been going very well lately. Can you lend me some money?"

Ready to eat!

Results are guaranteed!

I couldn't help feeling like something about Foxlyn's request wasn't quite right, but I always wanted to help a friend in need! So I searched through the pockets of my jacket, but all I found were:

- a **clothespin** for hanging laundry,
- a **candy** wrapper,
- and a **moldy cheese rind**.

I sighed. "I'm sorry — I'm low on money right now, too!"

Foxlyn knelt down and took the cheese rind that had fallen from my pocket. "Well, this is probably about ten years old . . . it could be worth something. If you don't need it, I'll take it!"

But as she was putting the cheese rind in her bag, something else fell out — a huge, *sparkly golden nugget*!

"Oops!" she cried, her fur turning even more red than usual. "Where did that come from?"

Cheesy creampuffs!

Winglet, Lorian, Dawn, Narek, and I exchanged confused looks. Could we TRUST our new travel buddy? Maybe we should be more careful.

As we continued along, the leaves around us began to clear until they disappeared entirely. The golden path went higher and higher, toward the sky, until it met up with a super ROCKY PEAK.

Oops!

# MOUSSSE, YOU'RE TOASSST!

We were so high up that the trees looked like little tufts of grass below, and the rivers like lines of silver drawn with a pencil. I was hanging on to the back of the dragon, while **Dawn** and WiNglet darted on beneath us. Luckily, they weren't afraid of heights — it

Yahooo!

actually seemed like they were
having fun running along the
GOLDEN PATH!

Lorian, who was riding the Emerald Dragon,
yelled down at Winglet, "Don't overdo it!"

In response, Winglet urged Dawn to run even
*FASTER*, yelling, "Yahoooo! Enjoy the view
for once and stop being so boring!"

Lorian made a face, but I could tell that he was urging Narek to **fly even faster**! Sigh! Why couldn't those two just work it out? And why didn't Blossom have me travel aboard a calm, super-slow sloth, instead of a powerful dragon?

Suddenly, the path split in two directions: on one side it headed into a **bramble bush** full of thorns, and on the other side it continued obstacle-free around the mountain.

Foxlyn said, "My gut, which is never wrong, tells me that we should take **that path**!" She pointed to the path without all the bramble bushes.

"I wish you were right," Lorian said seriously. "But the easiest path usually isn't the right one. There is only one way to know for sure: Winglet can use her mask again!"

As soon as Winglet saw us land, she put on the mask and looked around.

After a minute she shouted, "I see another key down there — it's hidden among the brambles! Lorian, pass me a CANE!"

The dragon tamer tossed it to her, and she easily caught it. Before I could twitch a whisker, she was making her way through the thorny shrubs.

"Here's another key!" she called. "This one isn't shaped like a spiderweb—"

"That's good news!" I cried.

"—but it is shaped like a snake!" Winglet finished.

"What?!" I stammered, trembling. That was definitely not good news!

We joined Winglet in the clearing that she had made between the bushes and spotted a rock that was blocking an opening in the mountain. It had a **LOCK**!

Winglet inserted the key and the rock moved, revealing a secret cave. Holey cheese, what an adventure! And it was about to get even crazier, because we saw what was hiding in the cave right away — **an enormouse monster**!

*Squeak!* It was a really long, slimy, terrifying snake, out of my **WORST** nightmares! Its coils could have strangled ten ogres at once, its scales

were as big as shields, but most importantly, it had **THREE HEADS**!

The path continued right under the snake's belly. If we wanted to get to the other side, we had to face it!

Quiet as mice, we tried to walk around the creature

without attracting attention, but the first head spotted us!

"Ssssistersss!" she hissed.

The second head opened her bright yellow EYES and cried, "Ssslurp, what luck! Today, once again, we feassst on ssssteamed moussse!"

The third head lifted up and said, "Tonight, I'm eating firssst! Yesssterday you gobbled almossst all that moussssse pie!"

Winglet faced them bravely and said, "I know that you want to have us for a snack, but we are on an important mission. We need to pass through your lair to bring life back to the Empire of Fantasy!"

The third head turned to her sisters. "Sssuch sass ssshe hasss! Viperette, Snakessa, what do you sssay?"

The three laughed, then Viperette said, "I think, dear Pythia, they should passs the tessst of the sssnakehisss!"

"Good idea!" Pythia agreed. "Our ssssister Snakessa can only say mostly words that use the letter *sss*! But sssince she's usssed almost all of them, she would like for you to sssuggest some new **combinationsss!**"

Snakessa smiled menacingly. "Surely, sssurprise us ssstrangers! Sssing sssonnets about sssnakes?!"

*A sonnet about snakes? Oh, for the love of all things cheesy!*

Winglet looked at me encouragingly. "Come on, Knight!"

I couldn't **disappoint** her, so I made up a little poem on the spot. (Hopefully, the snakes wouldn't realize that it wasn't a true sonnet!)

*Splendid sisters!*
*Shimmering stars!*
*Suave sparkles . . . and . . . and . . .*
*You seem to be such*
*succulent strawberries!*

I trembled from my tail
to my whiskers, waiting for
their response.

Viperette approved. "Well, thisss
isssn't bad!"

Snakessa agreed. "Sssufficient!
Surely sssincere!"

Pythia declared, "Sssoooo sssatisfactory:
You ssshall passs!"

I couldn't believe
it. I'D DONE IT!

**Hooray!**

We were so happy that even Winglet and Lorian **hugged** in celebration!

(Then they immediately separated, embarrassed.)

# THANKS FOR THE RIDE!

The second day of our journey was just about over by the time we left Viperette, Snakessa, and Pythia's lair. The path that took us to the ISLAND OF THE SEVEN SECRETS continued on the other side of the mountain and down into the valley.

Winglet continued along on Dawn, while Lorian, Foxlyn, and I followed on Narek's back. For once I forgot about my fear of heights and tried to enjoy flying along on the dragon's back . . . which swayed sweetly . . . maybe a bit too much . . . okay, maybe it was better to slow down a bit . . . just a little bit . . . it suddenly felt like we were on a roller coaster!

Help! Hang on tight!

GAME

What strange thing do you see near the dragon?

The answer is on page 144.

"HEEEEELP!" I yelled, clinging to Lorian's back. Why had Narek begun to fly so fast?

Glancing around, I suddenly understood — something was **pinching** his tail, and he was trying to get free!

When we saw what was happening, we were all speechless. Attached to Narek's tail was . . . a **TORTOISE**!

Lorian tried to calm the dragon. "I will free you, my friend! Hold the reins, Knight, while I try to figure out what's happening!"

Lorian climbed along the dragon's tail as I tried to take control. He reached his hand out to the tortoise and pulled her onto Narek's back.

We landed in a clearing next to the path. The tortoise climbed down veeery **SLOWLY**, coughed, and said, "Excuse me if I took advantage of the *ride*!"

* Answer to the game on page 142–143: There is a tortoise hanging on the dragon's tail.

Narek grumbled in response. His tail was as **SWOLLEN** as a bagpipe!

"A horse and carriage would have been more comfortable," the tortoise continued. "But sometimes, the important destinations aren't reached in a golden carriage, but on the back of a donkey! Right?"

"**Wise words,**" Lorian said, as if he had finally found someone who understood him.

Narek grumbled again, very offended. Lorian explained, "She didn't mean an actual donkey."

"Who are you?" Winglet asked. "And how did you end up hanging off the dragon's tail?"

The tortoise sighed. "I grabbed on when you left the monster's cave. You were my only hope of getting out of there! I was trying to find my way home, but I got lost — and ended up in that horrible cave!"

Holey cheese! I was pretty sure I'd seen the tortoise's shell in the middle of all those **skulls**!

"What a terrible place for a tortoise of my age!" she continued. "Oh, by the way, I'm **Creasely Wrinkledom**, countess of the ancient Diamond Shell lineage."

Lorian turned toward her. "Good to meet you. We are headed to the mysterious Island of the

# Creasely Wrinkledom

**Who:** The most ancient creature in the Kingdom of Fantasy. Her shell is made of many drawers, in which she keeps everything that could be useful to herself and to others, including her childhood memories. Day and night, she wears two large earrings as big as chandeliers. She never takes them off!

**Personality:** She is always very friendly but also isn't afraid to stand up for herself. She always has a pearl of wisdom to share, because even the most valiant heroes deserve a cuddle or a wise word every now and then!

**Her hobbies:** She loves singing in the moonlight!

Seven Secrets to bring the Empire of Fantasy back to life! We would be so pleased if you would come with us. After all, life is a journey, and those who travel live it twice!"

Winglet winked at me and whispered, "Hey, Lorian and Creasely really do have a lot in common!"

Creasely nodded. "Allow me to collect myself for a moment. After that journey, I feel a bit upside down!"

She touched the two golden earrings she was wearing, which were as big as chandeliers. "These are my prized possession. A very sweet friend, the baron Elden Tortoise, gave them to me. I never take them off!"

Then she whispered, "We were a formidable singing duo!"

She took a **photograph** out of one of the drawers in her shell. The photo showed her singing with a very elegant tortoise.

"Luckily," she added, tucking the photo away, "I never go anywhere without my makeup. *Voilà!*" She pulled a little mirror, a box of powder, and some **lipstick** from her shell.

"Would you like some, Knight?" she asked me. "You look so pale!"

"I suffer from dragon-sickness!" I admitted.

Creasely smiled. "Oh, you're sensitive, like many noble creatures!"

As Creasely told us more about her life as a noble tortoise, the sun set over the horizon. By now, the **THIRD DAY** had passed. We only had two days left to reach our destination.

"We need to hurry!" Foxlyn said. "Time is money!"

But we were all really tired and needed to rest. So we made up our beds for the night beneath a tree and lit a little fire. Winglet lay down next to Dawn, while Foxlyn told funny stories about her travels. Winglet was yawning, and Dawn was already sleeping!

I sat next to Lorian and Creasely, who were intent on roasting a few wild chestnuts for dinner.

"Between you and me, young man," Creasely said suddenly, with the voice of someone with centuries of experience, "even a blind bat could see that you and the princess care a lot for each other."

Lorian's face turned the color of fire.

"It's true," I added. "So why are you always so tough on Winglet?"

Lorian thought for a moment, then he said, "My job is to protect her. I have to prove myself worthy of that."

I nodded. "But maybe you could show her you care a bit more, too."

"There's a time to pick every fruit!" Creasely declared. "Don't let the apples fall with the lemons!"

Lorian and I looked at each other, confused. Even if her sayings were a bit odd, Creasely was really wise!

We fell asleep under a beautiful SUNSET.

# THE CARNIVOROUS
# SWAMP MONSTER

When I opened my eyes the next day, the sun was already high in the sky. We had all been so exhausted that we'd fallen into too deep a sleep!

"Those who snooze don't get the greens!" Creasely said, chewing loudly on a chunk of grass. "Would you like some?"

"Umm, no, thank you! I never eat salad for breakfast," I said politely. "Anyway, we need to get moving right away!"

We got our things together and continued on foot, full of energy, as Narek kept watch above us.

We followed the golden path past a hill. Slowly, the air became more and more humid, until it felt like we were in a sauna!

Soon we understood why — the path led us to the shores of a pond with **SWAMPY WATERS**. Winglet put on the Mask of the Winged Ones again, and it showed her a key hidden in a hollowed tree trunk. This time, it was shaped like a **FLAME**.

"What does fire have to do with anything?" I asked. "All I see around here is water!"

"There's a **LOCK** over here!" Winglet informed us, pointing to a small wooden door hidden in a tree. She put the key in, turned it, and the plants around us opened up like a curtain . . . but what waited for us on the other side was not at all enjoyable. In fact, it made my whiskers tremble in fright!

A shadow loomed over us. It was giant,

monstrous, as tall as a
mountain, and threatened
us with terrifying claws!

A deep voice thundered,
**"GOOOOO AWAAAAAY, WHILE
YOU STILL CAAAANNNNN!"**

What a fur-raising
fright!

"Speak up, I can't hear you!" Creasely said. "My hearing isn't always very good."

The shadow hesitated for a moment, and then responded, **"WHAAAAAT?"**

This time the voice echoed and rumbled even more deeply.

**"HOW DAAAARE YOU SPEAK THIS WAAAAAY TO THE SWAAAAAMP MOOOONSTER?"**

Always courageous, Winglet spoke up. "We don't mean to disrespect you! But if you could please let us pass, we must bring life back to the Empire of Fantasy and all its creatures, including you."

**"WHAAAAAT? YOU DON'T FEEEEEAR MEEEE?**

**YOU DON'T BEG ON YOUR KNEEEES FOR ME TO SPARE YOUR LIIIIVES?"**

Creasely moved over to me and whispered, "There's something about that shadow that doesn't convince me. It seems like he's doing

everything he can to scare us, but
I think it's all just talk!"

"You may be right!" I said,
even though my **FUR** was
ruffled in fear!

Just then, Lorian signaled
to us. He had gone behind a big
tree on the other side of the swamp.
Quiet as mice, we went around to
look — and what we saw left us
*speechless*!

# Never Trust
# Appearances!

Hidden behind the tree was a small, harmless tree frog!

The big shadow was a trick of lights and mirrors that made the frog seem enormouse!

As for her thundering voice, she was talking into tubes made from hollow branches. That's why it sounded so **deep**!

"Sooooo? I still haven't heard you begggg!" the harmless tree frog continued, not realizing that we were standing behind her.

Winglet tapped her on the back. "Knock, knock! The game's over. You've been discovered!"

"Aaaah!" the tree frog yelled, caught off guard. Then she frowned. "I knew that was a terrible swamp monster impression!"

"You can say
that again," Creasely
scolded, waving a wrinkly
foot at her.

"I don't know about that," Foxlyn put in. "She
actually has a sweet little voice! And she's so
teeny tiny . . . really anything but a swamp
monster!"

"It's never wise to trust appearances,"
Lorian remarked.

The tree frog's eyes, meanwhile, had begun to
tear up. In moments, she erupted into a

# FLOOD OF TEARS!

She was crying so much that a salty **puddle of water** was forming around our feet!

Sobbing, she said, "Oh, how humiliating! What a horrible failure! I've spent my whole life trying to **SCARE** people, just like the other guards, and now you've found me out. Oh, what a mess!"

I tried to make her feel better. "Oh, come on now, it's not that bad! You're being too hard on yourself!"

Chattering cheddar, I was trying to cheer up the **monster** that had threatened to eat us a moment earlier!

Waaaaaaaaaaahhhh!

But the tree frog continued to **cry** inconsolably. "My reputation is ruined! Finished! I'm just half a tadpole, an abandoned

**water lily**, leftover fly parts!"

Winglet bent down to hug her. "Don't say that!

*There's always hope!"*

Lorian also tried to lift her spirits. "Don't give up! We're here for you!"

Even Dawn rubbed up against the little frog, purring to comfort her.

The tree frog whimpered, "You can't possibly understand! The other **GUARDS** are so scary! Please don't tell anyone what a terrible job I did!"

"You have our word," Winglet promised. "We are going to leave now, and no one will know a thing. It will be our secret!"

Suddenly, the tree frog turned serious. "But I can't let you pass! I am still a **SWAMP GUARD**, and I must do my job."

Then she looked us in the eyes. "I'm sorry, but you'll have to pass the same test that awaits anyone who wants to pass:

THE FIRE JUMP!

It's my job to make you do it." She frowned. "And be careful. I saw a dragon flying in the sky — he is surely with you! Don't let him land, or I'll be forced to take action. Look what I can do!"

In a flash, the water of the pond caught fire. *Squeak!* A wave of heat scorched my whiskers!

# THE FIRE JUMP!

Lorian whistled to tell Narek to stay in the sky. Meanwhile, the pond had turned into a **POOL OF BURNING LAVA**. So that's why the key was shaped like a flame! My tail trembled in fright.

Like magic, many flat, round Leaves appeared on the surface of the pond, floating on the water like little rafts.

The tree frog explained, "To pass this test, you must get to the other side of the pond by jUMpinG on the lily pads, like this!"

She jumped from one leaf to the next, then turned to face us.

"That won't be too hard!" Winglet said. "It's just one step here, and then one there, and —"

The princess took her foot off the shore and placed it on the closest lily pad . . . but the lily pad sank down into the lava and **burned**! Winglet had to take a step back so she wouldn't fall in!

The tree frog shook her head. "You can't just step on the closest lily pad, Princess. You have to follow the exact **order** of my jumps!"

It burns!

Holey cheese, this was getting complicated!

"If you mess up even once, you'll fall into the lava!" the tree frog continued. "But if you manage to get across, not only will I let you pass, I'll give you my key for the next part of your journey. That's one of the Rules of the Swamp Guards!"

She waved an arm. "Now, enough chitchat — it's time to see if you have what it takes!"

Quick as a whip, the tree frog began to jump from one lily pad to the next, bouncing like a spring!

She jUMpeD in a ziGzaG so fast that my eyes

Follow the sequence!

crossed trying to watch her!

When she was on the other side, she gestured for us to follow her steps. "It's your turn!" she croaked.

My whiskers went limp. It was impossible to repeat that! Cheese and crackers, I didn't want to end up as **mouse fondue**!

Lorian stood tall and turned to Winglet. "If you will allow me, Princess, I will attempt to cross first. I watched the sequence carefully, and I think I can repeat it."

Winglet put her hands on her hips. "No way! I also watched *carefully*, and I know that I can lead us to the other side!"

Without waiting for an answer, she jumped on the first **lily pad**. It held her up — phew! It was the right one!

Then she hopped on the next, and that one didn't sink, either!

Then a third, then a fourth, and then a fifth . . .

Winglet went from one lily pad to the next. With every jump, my heart trembled like cheese pudding. I didn't know if the next step would be the right one . . . or be the end of her!

Lorian jumped on the first lily pad, and then it was my turn. *Squeak!* Dawn, Creasely, and Foxlyn followed me, while Narek flew over us, nervous because he couldn't help.

"Go slowly!" I begged. "I'm a bit out of shape!"

Cheesy creampuffs, even Creasely was more **FIT** than I was. "Come on, Knight!" she called from behind me. "I'm a few centuries older than you, but I can jump better!"

Winglet had almost arrived at the far side of the pond when she stopped. Oh no! Luckily, she remembered the pattern and kept going without sinking into the lava.

The princess couldn't allow herself a single

misstep! She didn't have far to go now.

But when Winglet jumped onto the last lily pad before reaching the opposite side of the pond, the lily pad **SANK**!

Holey cheese, it was the wrong one!

"Winglet!" Lorian cried. He jumped ahead and caught her before she fell into the lava! Carrying her, he jumped quickly from the lily pad to the far

Gotcha!

edge of the pond. She was **SAFE**!

I, on the other paw, was still quaking with fear!

Winglet and Lorian looked at each other for a moment. Then the princess jumped out of the **dragon tamer's** arms and said, "Thank you, but you shouldn't have. I would have been fine on my own!"

"I was just doing my job," Lorian said sadly.

I remembered what Blossom had said: Winglet could sometimes be too **proud**!

"Hooray!" the tree frog cheered as the rest of us reached the edge of the pond. "You did it! Well done!" Then she added, with pleading eyes, "Please take me with you! I am so done with this **SWAMP**! I want to come with you — that is, if you think I'm worthy . . . and if I won't be in the way . . . and if I'm not too small, or too green, or too —"

Winglet smiled. *"We'd love to have you!"*

# A SEA OF TROUBLE

Before we all set off again, the tree frog told us that her name was Mossy. She handed us the next precious key.

Winglet looked at it carefully. "It's decorated with a **shell**! No more spiderwebs, snake eyes, or flames. Maybe passing through this next part will be easier!"

Mossy was so happy to join us that she kept hopping around like crazy. "We're going to bring life back to the Empire of Fantasy!" she croaked. "If only the other guards knew I was helping with this brave **MISSION**! I will show them that I'm not marshland larva, a froggy wart, a —"

# Mossy

**Who:** One of the Swamp Guards, a lively tree frog with splendid emerald-green skin.

**Personality:** She seems calm and happy, but Mossy is actually very insecure and focuses a lot on her flaws, so she always feels out of place. She also seems to be hiding something . . .

**Her passions:** She loves chewy mud candies and has a passion for literature. Her favorite novels are *Froggy Karenina, Lord of the Flies, Lily Pad Heights,* and *The TreeTrothed.*

I put up a paw to stop her. "Don't start this again! Poor Mossy, I hope you'll gain some more confidence in yourself on this **adventure**."

As we continued along, the golden path led us to the middle of a very unusual-looking field. Instead of flowers, there were **silver bells** growing everywhere! They gently jingled in the breeze. I had to admit, it was a very pleasant and relaxing landscape, after all the dangers we had faced so far.

Next, we reached some **woods** that wrapped around a beach with the finest sand I'd ever seen. Around the base of the trees grew big, colorful mushrooms. But as we got closer, we discovered that they weren't mushrooms at all. They were slices of **bread** with **jam**!

"You can eat them!" Mossy reassured us. "These are very rare **Snack Trees** that grow along the path to refresh travelers!"

The bread and jam looked delicious, so we all enjoyed a few snacks — even Dawn and Narek!

The snacks seemed to recharge us and give us back our strength, after everything we'd been through so far.

"These are a real **treat**!" Winglet said, without looking at Lorian. "Flamelet would love them! She's so good at baking sweets. I'll save some for her. Maybe she can recreate the recipe when we get home!"

I enjoyed a moment of rest, but something wasn't right. I'm not a suspicious mouse, but I got the feeling that someone was **WATCHING** us . . . but who?

Creasely noticed that I was lost in thought. "You think too much!" she said sweetly. "Just enjoy your food! This is so exquisite that I think it cured my cold!"

After enjoying that tasty snack, we continued on our way.

We walked for hours and hours . . .

Then suddenly, the golden path dipped into the sea. It looked like we were supposed to walk right into the waves in order to continue!

But Foxlyn put up a paw. "We just ate! Can we still go in the water?"

Winglet smiled sadly. "My mom always says that, too — you should wait to go in the water after you've eaten." She frowned. "But that was hours ago and we can't waste any more time! We don't know how the battle against the **Invisibles** is going at Crystal Castle. We have to keep going . . ."

We were all a little unsure about getting in the water. I'm not a champion swimmer, after all!

"Don't be afraid," Mossy said. "You can *magically* breathe in these waters!"

So we all got completely under the water — even Narek!

*Come on, jump in!*

Suddenly, an incredible landscape appeared all around us. There were *amazing* creatures swimming everywhere!

I spotted a fish with wheels; a jellyfish that looked like a *ballerina* in a tutu; and a hammer fish followed by a fish shaped like a wrench, a *screwdriver* fish, and a bolt-shaped fish. How mouserifically strange!

"What world is this?" I asked Mossy, my eyes wide in astonishment. (I could even talk underwater!)

Mossy grinned. "It's the **Outlandish Ocean**!"

The little frog waved an arm all around us. "Creatures few have ever seen before live in this seabed."

"They are truly beautiful!" Winglet exclaimed.

## GAME
Can you count how many starfish there are in the sea?

The answer is on page 182.

"Yes," said Mossy. "But they can also be **SCARY**!"

I immediately began shaking from my ears to my tail. "Wh-what do you m-mean?"

Suddenly, in the darkness of the abyss below, I saw a light flicker on. It was getting closer, bigger, and more **blinding**.

"Look!" Foxlyn exclaimed, pointing. "Maybe it's a flashlight fish?"

"I don't think so," Mossy whispered. "It looks more like a Furnace Fish!"

CLING CLANG CLING CLANG
CLING CLANG CLING CLANG

What bone-chilling sounds! Creaking toward us like a rusty submarine was the scariest fish I'd ever seen. It looked like it was made out of **IRON**!

*The answer to the game on page 180–181 is four starfish.

It had a giant mouth, with teeth shaped like a bear trap and sparks of fire in its jaws! There was a white-hot lantern hanging from its head that left a trail of **FIERY BUBBLES** in its wake.

I was afraid this really was the end for us!

Creasely spoke up calmly. "It's best not to get too close to that beast! You can never be too *careful*."

"On the other paw," I squeaked, "You can never be too fearful! **HEEEELP!**"

Lorian drew his sword. "How can a fire stay lit underwater?"

"The waters of the Outlandish Ocean are one of a kind!" Mossy explained.

One thing was certain: The Outlandish Ocean had become a sea of trouble!

# A TREASURE TO PROTECT

The monster was getting closer and closer, so we quickly left the golden trail and hid in a sea cave. The **Furnace Fish** hurled himself against the rock that was protecting us and began to chew it to bits with its huge sharp teeth!

Creasely yelled, "It wants to eat us! Quick, everyone get in my shell!"

"You're very kind, but I'm afraid it's too tight of a fit," I objected.

The rock was beginning to **crumble**!

"This monster will eat us all," Lorian said. "We have to think of something — and fast!"

Winglet put the Mask of the Winged Ones over her face and saw that the golden path ended inside a giant shell.

"Quick!" she cried, pointing. "We need to follow the path to that giant **oyster shell**!"

We started to swim for our lives!

We got close to the shell and saw that there was treasure sparkling inside it: rubies, gold, sapphires, emeralds, topaz, and diamonds! The closer we got, the fiercer the Furnace Fish became. He was trying to defend the treasure!

The fish came toward us, yelling, "You cannot pass! I am the

GUARDIAN OF THE OUTLANDISH OCEAN TREASURE,

and I will not let you steal it!"

Then he opened his terrifying jaws, just to drive home his point. *Squeak!*

"We need to hurry!" Lorian cried. "We have to get to the path before the monster gets to us!"

It seemed impossible, because the fish was so fast, but we began to *wiggle* through the water as quickly as eels!

Even Creasely, who was usually pretty slow, pushed through those currents as fast as a catfish! (It was thanks to that bread and jam, which had really given us a *boost of energy*!)

We made it to safety inside the shell, but then realized that the path was blocked — by the treasure!

I tried to reason with the fish. "We would like to pass through here to continue on our way! But you have our word: We won't take even one *nugget of gold*."

Foxlyn seemed to disagree. Her eyes sparkled at the sight of all those riches!

"Mr. Guardian, look down there!" she cried

out, pointing randomly at the seabed.

The monster turned, and Foxlyn grabbed a handful of precious stones. The Furnace Fish noticed and roared, with a sound like clanging armor being crushed. "You wanted to cheat me right under my fins, YOU FOUL FOX? Now I'm going to turn you all into grilled meat!"

Guardian, look down there!

This really seemed like the end for us!

I was preparing for the worst when Foxlyn yelled, "No! I will give it all back, just don't touch my friends!"

The fox carefully put the precious stones back in their place.

"That's not good enough!" the monster roared.

Foxlyn held up her paws. "If you leave my friends alone, I will give you everything I own — everything I've earned my whole life!"

In front of our eyes, she emptied the bag she carried around her waist. A waterfall of golden nuggets fell out!

The monster's eyes sparked with admiration, but not because of the gold. "You care a lot about your friends, fox!" he gurgled. "You put them ahead of your love of gold. I WILL LET YOU PASS!"

Foxlyn had sacrificed her entire savings to help us. I was touched! I am a very sentimental mouse, after all.

"We are so grateful, Furnace Fish," Winglet

said. "I will remember this forever. Thanks to you, we will bring life back to the Empire of Fantasy!"

Suddenly, as if by magic, the golden path reappeared. We were ready to continue our voyage, our **hearts** filled with gratitude!

We were about to leave when we heard a creaking at our backs. The Furnace Fish was wailing and **CRYING OUT IN PAIN**!

"It has been such a long time since I have met anyone with such a pure heart!" he said. "Everyone is always trying to snatch my gold! Please, fox, stay and keep me company. I feel so alone in this freezing abyss!"

# THE SPHINX
# CHALLENGE

Foxlyn looked at us, confused. She hadn't planned to move to the bottom of the sea, but the Furnace Fish was so **sad**.

"Okay, I will stay," Foxlyn agreed finally. "But just for a *little while*!"

I hugged her. "We will come back to get you, oh NOBLE Foxlyn! You have the Fearless Knight's word!"

Mossy hugged her and said, "When we see each other again, I will buy one of those self-confidence classes from you!"

Even Creasely hugged her and said, "You have truly surprised me. Even the roughest rock can hide a precious stone."

"Well said," agreed the Furnace Fish. "And to

thank you for bringing me a new friend, I will give you a gift for your trip." He took a *golden nugget* from Foxlyn's bag. It lit up like a star! "This nugget represents Foxlyn's pure heart.

I will give you a gift for your trip!

Thank you!

Only the **gold of the noble spirit** will allow you to reach the Island of the Seven Secrets."

Wow — I was squeakless!

"When the time is right, toss the nugget into the *cloud lake* that surrounds the island," the Furnace Fish went on. "Then help will appear on the shore."

"You take it," Winglet said, nodding at me. "I trust you to carry the special nugget."

I held the nugget between my paws. As we followed the path in the shell, I shed a **TEAR**!

Foxlyn shouted good-bye, waving a paw. "Come back soon!"

The path picked up on the other side of the sea, along a stretch of grass that had been matted down by the wind. We kept walking slowly, because we were sad to leave a friend behind. Winglet and Lorian had even stopped arguing! We would all really miss Foxlyn.

A pinkish light filled the DAWN sky. Another day had passed while we were underwater. We had so little time left to get the crown!

As we continued, the wind grew stronger and stronger. I had to hold on to Narek so that I wouldn't FLY away like a leaf! Suddenly, the path ended at the edge of a cliff. Squeak, we were so, so, so, so, so, so, so high up!

It was time to put on the mask again. Winglet saw that, just one step before the cliff's edge, there was a new key. This time, the key was shaped like the outline of a wing.

Lorian waved for Narek to land nearby and said, "The wing is a symbol of the air. Maybe we need to look for the next opening up in the sky."

Winglet held the key out in front of her, in the

empty air. As if by magic, the path appeared again! It continued over the cliff toward the horizon!

Dawn jumped onto the path fearlessly, but just then, a loud shriek echoed through the air.

Above us, a winged animal was flying. It looked like a jumble of different monsters: It had the wings of an eagle, the body of a lion, and the head of a hawk!

"I am the Wind Sphinx!" it yelled. "Now you will taste my claws!"

"And you will taste my purse!" Creasely replied bravely, pulling a bag out of her shell and waving it around. "Stay back! Does that seem like the way to speak to a lady?"

Lorian asked Narek to leave Mossy, Creasely, and me next to Winglet. Then he said, "Protect the princess on our mission, Knight, while I go face this creature!" Then Lorian and Narek took off into the sky to begin their BATTLE.

Winglet hollered after them, "Lorian, now you are making me mad! I won't let you do this alone!"

She reached for her bow and arrow, but they weren't there. They had **disappeared**! She must have lost them in the Outlandish Ocean!

"Nooo!" she cried, upset.

"We won't leave you here, **LORIAN**!" I said, trying to stop our friend.

Lorian called back, "The sun on this fifth day is about to set. We only have a couple of hours before we lose every hope of finding the crown! Go! Do it for the Empire of Fantasy!"

"No!" Winglet yelled again.

Lorian looked down at her calmly. "This has always been my mission, Princess: TO PROTECT YOU!"

Lorian disappeared beyond the clouds. We could only hear the cries of the dragon and the Wind Sphinx as they **FOUGHT** higher and higher in the sky.

# REBEL TEARS

**W**inglet continued to shout his name.

But Lorian didn't respond, even when the noises from the battle above us had stopped.

My **heart** was broken. It wasn't possible that Lorian had sacrificed himself for the mission, was it? I couldn't believe I had lost such a courageous and wise friend!

Dawn kept walking along the golden path, carrying us on her back. "I can't believe it," the princess said between sobs. "I have been so unfair to Lorian! He has always been so caring, and I was horrible in return. Since we were **little**, he tried to teach me what to do, how to *shoot a bow and arrow*, even how to breathe. He was the best!"

Like this!

"You cared for him a great deal," Creasely said.

"I did," Winglet admitted sadly. "But I never told him how much he meant to me." She sighed heavily, tears rolling down her cheeks. "You don't know what you have until it's gone."

Poor Winglet!

I couldn't bear to see her with a broken heart!

"Don't worry," I said. "I am sure that Lorian and Narek will beat that monster!"

"The knight is right," Creasely said. "When I was just a little more than

Ommmm . . .

a century old, I felt just like you. But now that I'm a few years older, I can say that I can recognize a **brave knight** when I see one. Lorian is definitely it!"

Winglet took a deep breath.

Creasely added, "I also know a courageous princess when I see one, and you are definitely it, Winglet."

"Yes!" I cheered. "And now you need to concentrate on our mission. Do it for your mother, and for Lorian! After all, aren't you the **Rebel Princess**?"

Winglet looked deep into our eyes, then she wiped away her tears. "You're right — I can't stop now. Dawn, let's go!

*The crown awaits!*"

# A MYSTERIOUS FIGURE

Winglet climbed on Dawn's back, but just as we were about to continue, we noticed that someone was missing: Mossy!

In the confusion of the battle, we hadn't noticed that she was gone!

Suddenly, boing! The tree frog leaped up onto the path. "Here I am, friends! Sorry that I disappeared, but that sphinx scared me!" she said, embarrassed.

Here I am, friends!

Well, she wasn't exactly a great example of courage, but who was I to judge? I'm the biggest 'fraidy mouse of all! I smiled and said, "The

DANGER has passed, you don't have to be scared!"

We all continued along the path for a while, until we reached the other side, safe and sound. In the blink of an eye we were standing in front of an island surrounded by a *cloud lake*!

We looked at one another in shock. We had finally found the mythical and legendary

## ISLAND OF tHE SEVEN SECRETS!

"But . . . you can't see a cheese rind!" I squeaked.

The fog around the lake was very thick. How in the name of cheese would we ever manage to cross it?

"The *golden nugget* from the Furnace Fish!" Winglet said with a gasp. "Remember? We need to toss it in the cloud lake, and it will help us pass."

I searched my pockets and pulled it out. For a moment, I couldn't help thinking of our friend

## GAME

There are dangers
hidden in the fog. Can
you see them?
The answer is on
page 208.

Foxlyn, hanging out with fish at the bottom of the *sea*.

I was about to toss the nugget into the lake . . . when someone grabbed it from my paw!

I turned. Standing behind me was a creepy **hooded figure**. She was surrounded by three spears that looked like they were suspended in midair! There was no doubt about it: Those were

# THE INVISIBILE WARRIORS!

The figure's voice was cold. "I will take this nugget. Go back where you came from, rat, and no one will get hurt."

Winglet came to my defense. "He's not a rat, he is the Fearless Knight! And you aren't worth one of his whiskers. LET HIM GO!"

The hooded figure did not show her face, but I could hear her evil laugh. Then she added, "You

---

*Answer to the game on page 206–207: If you take a good look around the mountain's peak, you can see six spears belonging to the Invisible Army hidden in the fog.

poor heroes! I'm almost touched. You never seem to know when it's the right time to give up and save your fur! GUARDS, STOP HER!"

"Don't touch the princess, or you'll have to deal with me!" I said. But I didn't scare them too much, because the third spear stuck out and tripped me. I TUMBLED right onto my snout!

Just then, Mossy began jUMpinG all around the enemy. Was it a trick to distract them?

"MASTER!" croaked the tree frog. "Did I do a good job?"

The hooded figure barely looked at the frog. "Mmm-hmm, yes, you blabbered about the secret of the golden nugget, and you made Winglet lose track of her bow and arrow . . . even though

I had to do all the rest!"

"Wait — what?! The nugget? The bow and arrows?" I asked, surprised.

Mossy grinned. "I took them when you were all paying **aᴛᴛeᴨᴛioᴨ** to the Furnace Fish. Now they're at the bottom of Outlandish Ocean!"

So that's where they had gone. Holey cheese, I couldn't believe my ears!

"**You are a traitor!**" Creasely yelled. "I always thought you were hiding something! I knew we couldn't trust you! That's why I kept feeling like someone was following us — they were!"

"I did a good job, then!" the tree frog cheered, turning back to the hooded figure. "Now will you turn me into a creature who is majestic, powerful, and terrifying, just like the other **GUARDS**?!" Mossy said. She jumped all around, impatient to get her prize.

"No, you proved yourself to be just what I

always thought you were: a useless tree frog!" the mysterious figure hissed as she carelessly tossed Mossy aside.

Then she turned toward the cloud lake and tossed in the golden nugget. As soon as it landed,

a **rowboat** appeared on the shore.

The mysterious figure climbed in, but first she turned and ordered the Invisibles, "Take care of those pests while I go get what is waiting for me: the **Crown of the Empire**!"

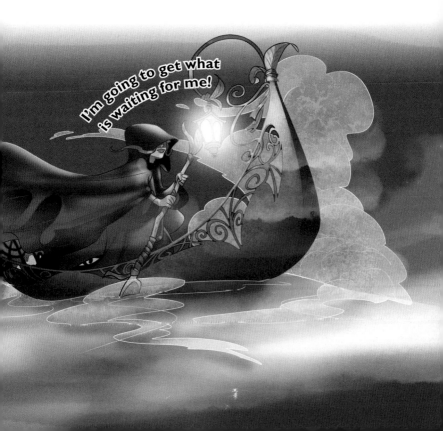

# THE NOBLE SPIRIT'S GOLD

As the figure rowed away, the three Invisibles made themselves visible and pointed their rusty spears at us.

Rats! They really were gray, gloomy, and scary. I felt my knees turn as wobbly as ricotta cheese!

"So, here we are at a showdown with the Rebel Princess," grumbled one of the soldiers.

"Let's see how you manage without your bow!" another one challenged.

Winglet wasn't scared. She grabbed a stick and used it to BATTLE the Invisibles!

They were strong and sneaky — they would disappear suddenly and reappear in another spot altogether.

"Here I am!"

"No, here!"

"Now I'm here!"

Winglet blocked the spears' blows and **attacked** with quick moves. But she couldn't manage alone against three enemies!

Dawn jumped in to help, knocking a **warrior** over with her big paws.

Finally, I can see you!

**Creasely** and I needed to help, too! So Creasely tucked her head and her paws in her shell. I lifted her up and . . . *TOSSED* her right at the head of one of the Invisibles!

"We did it!" we all cheered. Together, Winglet and Dawn had managed to knock out the other two Invisibles . . . but Winglet had been hit, too. She was **UNCONSCIOUS**!

I lifted her up carefully and carried her to the lake. "Quick, we need to get her to the island before the enemy takes the crown!"

"But how can we manage without the golden nugget?" Creasely asked. "The lake is just a **giant cloud**!"

Rats, she was right! I sat on the shore of the lake, laying the princess down next to me. She had fought with such courage. Was it all for nothing?

"I've let Blossom down! I didn't help Winglet reach her destination. The Empire of Fantasy is lost forever!" I squeaked in desperation.

Creasely looked at me sweetly and took off one of her *precious earrings*.

"These aren't real gold, you know," she confided. "But they are the most precious thing I own. I will gladly give them to you, for Winglet's sake. Maybe they'll work on the lake!"

I was moved by the offer! "Maybe they aren't

worth a lot of money, but the Furnace Fish said that only the **gold of the noble spirit** will allow us to reach the Island of the Seven Secrets," I said. "You definitely have a noble spirit. It's worth a try!"

Creasely let one of the earrings fall into the lake. A second later, another rowboat magically appeared on the shore, surrounded by fog.

"**Thank you, my friend!**" I cried happily. "Quick, let's get in the boat!"

But Creasely stayed put. "You go, Knight. This is Winglet's challenge, and she'll need your help. Dawn and I will wait here and fight off these beasts for as long as we can."

"I can't thank you both enough," I said to Creasely and Dawn, hugging them. "We will be back — with the Crown of the Empire!"

I carefully placed Winglet into the boat and began to **row** toward the island.

By the time we got close to our destination, Winglet was still out cold. I tried to *wake her*.

"Princess, we are approaching the island!" I whispered, shaking her shoulder gently.

Winglet slowly opened her eyes. First she looked at me, and then she looked around me.

"Knight? Where are we? Ohhhh. . ." she muttered, looking at the scene in front of us.

She couldn't manage to sit up, but she called out, "Quick, Knight, let's go get the Crown of the Empire and rescue the kingdom!" She paused. "But where are Dawn and Creasely?"

"Our friends stayed on the shore to fight off the

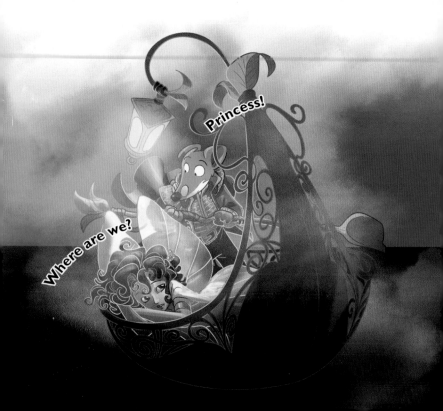

Invisibles," I explained.

We had traveled all night. When we finally pulled the **BOAT** onto the island's shore, we found an unexpected land before us. I had imagined a lush green island, filled with colorful plants and beautiful animals. But there were no trees, flowers, shrubs, leaves, blades of grass, moss, mushrooms, roots, or cacti. I didn't see a single bird, insect, cow, owl, giraffe, zebra, or any other creature at all, for that matter. This mythical island just looked like a **ROCK** planted in the middle of a cloudy sea!

Right in the middle of the rocky island, we could see a pointy mountain surrounded by a stretch of bare land.

"Let's go explore!" Winglet proposed, seeming to feel better by the moment. "We need to hurry and find the crown!"

# A BITTER SURPRISE

We had finally gotten to the island. But we still didn't have any idea how to find the mythical crown! Around us, all we could see were stones, rocks, mountains, cliffs, and spiky, rocky peaks. Rats, now what?

Winglet pointed to the mountain at the center of the island. "I think we should go over there."

I could see that it would be a long walk! The mountain was sharp and . .

## SO SUPER STEEP!

My paws ached, my eyes were half-closed with exhaustion, and all of the BONES in my body hurt — but I would never abandon the princess.

So just like that, we headed off together toward

the mountain. But after a short while, we were met with a **TERRIBLE SURPRISE** — the hooded figure in the long, rustling cloak was headed there, too!

"Hey!" Winglet called to her. "Why did you attack me?"

The figure turned, furious. "You!

## HOW DID YOU MANAGE TO GET HERE?"

"I'm here thanks to something that you surely know nothing about," Winglet said, "my friendship with the heroes who have given their hearts to this mission!"

"Friendship is just an obstacle on the road to success," the mysterious figure sneered.

"Oh, yeah?" Winglet cried. "At least have the courage to **SHOW YOUR FACE**!"

The figure slowly pulled her hood back, saying,

"As you wish . . . my friend."

Holey cheese — it was *Flamelet*, Winglet's friend!

The princess gasped. "This is not possible!"

Flamelet smiled. "Oh, yes it is! They call you the Rebel Princess, but you are so young

That's not possible!

What?!

and sweet that it was easy to gain your trust and pretend to be your **friend**!"

How dare she talk to Winglet like that?

The princess's face blazed red with rage. "You were my friend! I

Yes, it's really me

took you in at Crystal Castle like a sister . . . and you **BETRAYED** me!"

"A sister? Let's not get carried away," Flamelet said with a smirk. "I would say more like . . . a **cousin**!"

For the love of cheese! As she spoke, Flamelet's face had changed!

"I can finally go back to my **REAL APPEARANCE**," she said, satisfied.

Here's my real face!

"But I don't have any cousins!" Winglet objected.

"That's where you're wrong," Flamelet said. "I am the daughter of **WITHER**, your mother's evil twin sister. I am your cousin!"

"But how? Why?" Winglet stammered, confused.

"My mother knew that the Invisibles would attack and figured that the Legend of the Empire would come true," Flamelet explained. "She made me *sneak* into Crystal Castle to steal the Mask of the Winged Ones so that she could use it to find the crown. But I couldn't get my hands on it, so I had to follow you to find the island." She gave a wicked grin. "You did all the hard work, and I'll get the **crown**!"

Winglet couldn't believe her ears. "You're right, I was naïve. At least now I know why I felt such instant **affection** toward you, as if I had known you forever. We're cousins!"

Flamelet nodded. "And thanks to our bond, I was able to give you that!" she said, pointing to the dragonfly *barrette* Winglet always wore in her hair.

Winglet reached up to touch it, looking even more shocked.

"It's *magical* — I just had to follow its trail to find you," Flamelet revealed. "Then that silly frog did the rest, showing me the secret of the nugget . . . and here I am!"

"Nothing is as it seems," the princess said, overcome with sadness as she took the clip out of her hair. "Not even the GIFT you gave me . . ."

Poor Winglet! Her whole world had been shattered into a thousand pieces!

"It seems you're finally beginning to understand," Flamelet said. "My mother and I will take that crown. Then, with the Invisible Army, we will reestablish the Empire of Fantasy — in the service of **EVIL**!"

Winglet's eyes flashed. "You'll never do that as long as I'm here!"

"Step aside, Winglet," Flamelet warned. "I have already won!"

a voice thundered.

*Squeak!* I looked around, but didn't see anyone. Who said that?

# THE ROCK GIANT

The princess asked, "Who is it . . . is it . . . is it?"

The island was so deserted that Winglet's voice echoed through the valleys, rolled down the hills, and jumped from the rocks!

**Ba-bum, ba-bum, ba-bum, ba-bum, ba-bum, ba-bum!**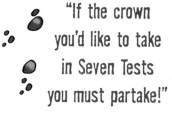

"What was that?" asked Flamelet.

"Umm, that's my heartbeat," I squeaked up, embarrassed. "I'm a bit scared!"

Just then, the voice thundered once more:

"If the crown
you'd like to take
in Seven Tests
you must partake!"

The voice was so deep that the ground cracked beneath my paws! Cheesy creampuffs!

"Who said that . . . at . . . at . . . at?" Winglet asked.

As far as I could tell, there was no one on the island except for Winglet, Flamelet, and me. There was nothing around except for the **HUGE MOUNTAIN** towering over us, with its rocky walls, its rough hands, its big eyes, and —

Holey cheese! Wait a minute, right in front of us was a . . .

We didn't realize before because it blended right into the side of the mountain!

As he began to approach us, I felt every strand of my fur tremble with fear!

## GAME

Can you see the rock giant?

The answer is on page 238.

Have you ever seen a mountain bend over? Well, that's exactly what the giant did to introduce himself!

"Elegant warriors, maidens grand,
I welcome you to my barren land.
This land you walk is rugged and rough,
everything here is sharp-edged and tough.
Only from rock, with its severity and weight,
can come strength and all things truly great.
I know not much about animals or plants
since here, on my island, those things
are quite scant.
So I hope my asking is not amiss,
but what funny sort of thing is this?"

With that, he grabbed me by my tail with his huge rock fingers and **LIFTED ME HIGH IN THE SKY**!

*Answer to the game on page 236–237: The giant is on the right side of the image, where the waterfall is.

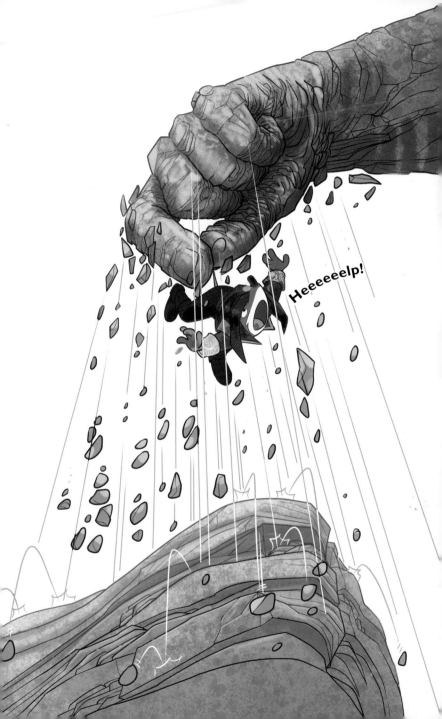

"Please, giant, put me down!" I squeaked. "I'm afraid of heights! And — oh! — I'm a mouse!"

"I am *Flamelet*," Wither's daughter interrupted, jumping in front of Winglet. "And I am here to take the Crown of the Empire!"

"I am Winglet," the princess cut in proudly. "I, too, am here to take the Crown of the Empire!"

The giant placed me gently on the ground and announced:

"This is where the tough path starts
to get the crown you want with all your heart.
Seven tests you must withstand,
and only one will win command.
Give it your all and let your heart sing,
be strong and brave: May the best one win!"

# PRINCESS CHESS

At that moment, a **CHESSBOARD** appeared in front of Winglet and Flamelet. I was trembling from the tip of my tail to the ends of my ears. I hoped that my dear friend Winglet would win!

The giant went on:

> "Let's get the first test underway,
> It tests intelligence and strategy.
> Each time your opponent takes your piece,
> a warrior he looks like will then cease!"

What in the name of cheese did that mean? This giant spoke in *riddles*!

But when I looked at the chessboard, I knew just what he meant. Holey cheese! The black pieces

looked like the Invisibles, while the white ones looked like the Winged Ones!

Each time Winglet or Flamelet overpowered the other's piece, the warrior that it depicted would disappear in real life! Rats, what horror!

Arthur Kindheart

Winglet moved first. "This piece represents Arthur Kindheart, a guard at the castle who has always been good to me," she told me.

Flamelet knocked away that piece almost immediately, moving an Invisible solider piece that had *Longsword the Hideous* written on it.

Longsword the Hideous

Winglet shuddered and

responded with a move.

"Take that!" Flamelet said, knocking down a tower that looked like Winky Bluefur!

"And you take that!" Winglet said as she took one of the black bishops labeled Lieutenant Destructo.

Then, with the Bishop Sterling of the Silver Dragons, Winglet took out the black knight (Temperton Bellyache), but it wasn't enough.

Soon Winglet was winning, but she hurt with every loss. She was playing to save her pieces, while Flamelet was attacking — after all, she had no fear of losing!

Temperton Bellyache

Sterling of the Silver Dragons

"Be strong, Princess. Don't give up!" I said.

Soon, Flamelet's pieces had surrounded the piece that Winglet cared about most of all: *Blossom*!

She smiled triumphantly, about to take the queen, but Winglet simply couldn't allow it.

She stood up and cried, "Enough! I surrender! You win!"

Winglet was inconsolable over the pieces she had lost. We weren't sure if any danger had come

Winglet, stay calm!

to those people in real life!

I ran to **comfort** her.

"Knight," Winglet said to me with tears in her eyes, "this isn't going very well!"

"It was a tough challenge," I said. "But it is just the first of SEVEN TESTS. Don't lose hope!"

Then the giant announced:

"The first test was won by Flamelet!
Now to the next task we must get.
You must concentrate and take it slow
as you aim at the target with your arrow and bow!"

# You'll Win with Your Eyes Closed!

A **TARGET**, like the ones that Winglet used at Crystal Castle, suddenly appeared.

"A bow and arrow!" I said. "This is your specialty, Princess! You'll win this one with your eyes closed!"

The giant boomed:

"A great idea, mouse — they'll close their eyes!
Hitting the target will bring them closer to the prize.
Victory goes to the one who can concentrate right
and hit the bull's-eye . . . but without sight!"

"Oh, no, that's not what I meant. That's just a thing people say!" I tried to explain. "You shouldn't listen to me!"

"Don't worry, Knight," Winglet assured me, winking. "I can do it!"

But as she spoke, the target moved — it actually began to jUMp around! Holey cheese, this just got extra tricky!

Two bows and three arrows each appeared at Winglet's and Flamelet's feet. The giant said:

"Hit the target that jumps here and there. You'll only get three chances — so take good care!"

Blindfolds ✚ jumping target ✚ anxiety ✚ only three chances = **IMPOSSIBLE**! Rats, this was tough!

The giant put two blindfolds in my paws so that I could cover Winglet's and Flamelet's eyes. Flamelet got to go first, since she had won the first test.

She pulled the BOW, took a deep breath, and whispered to Winglet, "Watch and learn!"

The first ⇒ *arrow* ➔ zoomed through the air and skidded off a rock; the second ended up in a crack in the ground; and the third missed the target by a hair, but didn't hit the bull's-eye! Phew!

"It's your turn, Princess!" I shouted. "Give it everything you've got!"

Winglet took a deep breath, pulled the bow, and launched all three arrows in a row. *Thwong!*

Hooray! Three perfect hits!

*Thwong! Thwong!*

There was a moment of silence . . .

Then Winglet pulled off the **blindfold** and cheered, "Hooray! I won! Three perfect hits!"

# THE WILDEBEEST MOVE

I was bursting out of my fur with excitement! "How did you do it?" I asked Winglet.

She smiled at me. "I remembered my training sessions with Lorian."

I had to smile at that. "Lorian would have been really proud of you!" I told her.

The giant named the winner of the second test and announced the third.

"The winner of that test is Princess Winglet,
who has proven she can get the perfect hit!
But now the third test will be won
by the competitor who has the balance to get it done."

The ground around us suddenly split and

252

POLES shot out, reaching toward the sky.
*Squeak!*

They were so many poles, it seemed like a
forest!

"Your martial arts battle will be up where it's tall;
Don't use your wings — with those you may fall!
Your true support won't be your feet,
but instead your hidden balance that can't be beat."

This giant was so puzzling! I
didn't understand a single cheese
curd of what he said! All I

But they're
so tall!

**Hold tight, if you can!**

knew for sure was that the poles were too thin and narrow for anyone to keep their **BALANCE** on for long!

Luckily, the giant's heart wasn't made of stone (unlike the rest of him!), so he made a **pool of water** appear beneath the poles. That way, whoever fell would just take a nice swim!

While my brain was busy bouncing from one thought to another, Winglet had already climbed to the top of one of the poles! She was keeping her **BALANCE** as she prepared to take on Flamelet.

Flamelet attacked first, trying to scare her. "See if you can withstand this **whale blow**!"

But Winglet jumped to another pole and returned the blow.

Flamelet fought back. "Take this **WILDEBEEST MOVE**!"

Winglet laughed. "So many names — it seems like you have a black belt in chattering!"

But even with all the chatting, Flamelet was holding her own! She made one move, then Winglet did. From the ground, it seemed like a mysterious dance of blows and blocks, attacks and defenses!

After this had gone on for a while, Flamelet

looked down and yelled in fear, "Oh no! Knight!"

Surprised, Winglet looked down. It was just one of Flamelet's **tricks** to confuse her — but it worked!

Winglet swayed . . . wobbled . . . teetered . . . faltered . . .

Cheese and crackers, she was about to FALL!

*Hold tight, Winglet!* I thought, concentrating as hard as I could. And it worked!

At the last moment, Winglet took a deep **breath**, calmed down, and found her **BALANCE**!

Furious, Flamelet tried to hit her harder, but she missed and lost her balance. She fell into the water with a loud *splash*!

"Hooray! Hooray!" I yelled, jumping with joy. The **Rebel Princess** had won the third test!

# THAT'S NOT FAIR!

Flamelet came out of the water completely **SOAKED**, her hair stuck to her head like an algae hat! Then the giant remarked:

"The princess has now taken the lead.
Don't get mad, Flamelet, have courage indeed!
You must concentrate a little bit more
instead of making up whales, wildebeests,
and other lore!"

"Don't do a victory dance yet," Winglet's cousin hissed at her, **WRINGING OUT** her wet cloak. "There are still four tests to go!"

My whiskers were trembling with stress!

Who knew what challenge awaited! What would it be? I was impatient to find out!

The giant soon answered my question:

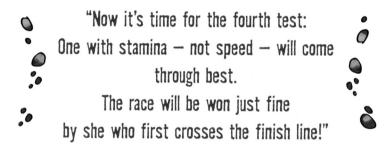

"Now it's time for the fourth test:
One with stamina — not speed — will come through best.
The race will be won just fine
by she who first crosses the finish line!"

A twisty track appeared in front of Flamelet and Winglet that ran the length of the island. They would have to compete in a looong *RACE*!

And, of course, the task of starting the race was given to . . . me!

The giant handed me a huge gong. When I banged it, the competitors would begin!

I cried, "Ready, set . . . go!"

I hit the **GONG** as hard as I could.

Both Winglet and Flamelet ran as fast as **LIGHTNING**! The giant invited me to sit on his shoulder so I could see the race from above. It was a bit too high for my taste — I'm too fond of my fur! — but I had to admit, it was a great view!

Flamelet started out **superfast**. She was upset and wanted payback!

But Winglet, who ran more steadily, took the lead after two curves!

"WING-LET! WING-LET!" I chanted.

She was about to cross the finish line! But just then, Flamelet jumped off the track and cut down a side street. No fair! That was a SHORTCUT!

A few moments later, she quickly popped back onto the main course, passed Winglet, and cried, "I am the Winner!"

She had crossed the finish line before the princess!

"That's not fair!" I protested, pointing a paw. "She cheated!"

# Responsibility and Wisdom

The giant ignored me and went on to announce the **FIFTH TEST**. Rats! Winglet was just going to have to win the next one.

"In the fifth test, the things that are key
are wisdom and responsibility!
The one to take the crown and the power
must be filled with knowledge at every hour.
In this test, you must display
the good sense and judgment you need to reign!"

This time, a ledger with a $\boxed{B}\boxed{O}\boxed{O}\boxed{K}$ on it appeared before the competitors. Winglet and Flamelet read it and reflected in silence.

YOU ARE EMPRESS.
BUT BECAUSE OF A FAMINE, YOUR
PEOPLE ARE STARVING!
A WIZARD DECIDES TO HELP YOU
AND GIVES YOU THREE GIFTS: A
THOUSAND LOAVES OF BREAD,
A GRAIN, AND A SONG. YOU
MUST PUT THEM IN ORDER OF
IMPORTANCE. WHICH IS IT?

Then *Flamelet* said, "First, a thousand loaves of bread to feed the hungry people! Then the grain to make bread, so they won't go hungry in the future, and finally a song. After all, what would you need a song for if people are hungry?"

Winglet listened. Then she said thoughtfully, "I would do the reverse. First the song, then the grain, and finally the thousand loaves. The **song** helps to lift people's spirits while waiting for the grain to grow, makes them feel happy, and stops them from starting wars because of their hunger. The **thousand loaves** would come last, since those would fill their stomachs in the moment, but not in the future."

## DO YOU REALLY KNOW THE KINGDOM OF FANTASY?

1. WHAT IS THE NAME OF THE PASSAGE THAT LEADS TO THE COUNTY OF THE BLUE WEASELS?

    A. THE ARCHWAY OF PERENNIAL SNOW

    B. THE ICE PASSAGE

    C. THE DOOR TO ETERNAL WINTER

2. WHERE, IN THE KINGDOM OF THE SEA, IS ANCHOVY VILLAGE LOCATED?

    A. IN THE SECRET LAIR OF THE MORAY EELS

    B. IN FLYING SQUID FOREST

    C. NEXT TO DARTING EEL FALLS

# GAME

Help Winglet answer the questions!

The answers are on page 269.

3. WHAT IS THE NAME OF THE LAST GIANT (MADE OF FLESH. NOT STONE. AND IS NONE OTHER THAN THE COUSIN OF THIS HERE KEEPER OF THE CROWN)?

A. STRONGHEART

B. HEARTBREAK

C. HEARTBEAT

4. WHAT IS HIS WIFE'S NAME?

A. HILDEGARDE PINCHLAQUER

B. BEATRICE BIGFOOT

C. THERESA STAMMERTOES

5. WHAT ARE THE STINKIEST CREATURES IN THE KINGDOM OF FANTASY CALLED?

A. STINKHEELS

B. GORGONZOIDS

C. TROLLS

DO YOU REALLY KNOW THE
KINGDOM OF FANTASY?

1. WHAT IS THE NAME OF THE PASSAGE THAT LEADS TO
THE COUNTY OF THE BLUE WEASELS?
A. THE ARCHWAY OF PERENNIAL SNOW
B. THE ICE PASSAGE
C. THE DOOR TO ETERNAL WINTER

2. WHERE, IN THE KINGDOM OF THE SEA, IS ANCHOVY
VILLAGE LOCATED?
A. IN THE SECRET LAIR OF THE MORAY EELS
B. IN JETTING SQUID FOREST
C. NEXT TO DARTING EEL FALLS

3. WHAT IS THE NAME OF THE LAST GIANT
(MADE OF FLESH, NOT STONE, AND IS NONE
OTHER THAN THE COUSIN OF THIS HERE
KEEPER OF THE CROWN)?
A. STRONGHEART
B. HEARTBREAK
C. HEARTBEAT

4. WHAT IS HIS WIFE'S NAME?
A. HILDEGARDE PINCHLAQUER
B. BEATRICE BIGFOOT
C. ...

5. WHAT A...

**I don't know this one . . .**

**The answer is easy!**

The giant did not say anything yet. He merely turned the page of the book to reveal a **TEST** about the Kingdom of Fantasy!

Winglet and Flamelet answered the questions one by one, thinking about each question.

When they were done, the giant analyzed their answers and said:

"The fifth test has been won by Winglet, who showed great wisdom with the order she set. Flamelet instead has won number six responding correctly and responding quick. Only those who know their land are worthy to run it and make it the best!"

Oh, for the love of cheese, the princess and her cousin were **TIED**! This competition was getting so intense, I was tying my tail in knots!

*Answer to the game on page 266–267: 1-C, 2-A, 3-A, 4-B, 5-C.

# Hang on to Me!

Suddenly, we heard the loud sound of a cornet. The giant was blowing into it with all his might to announce the seventh and final test!

What fear! What fright! I didn't even get this worked up when I was named the Fearless Knight! After all, this time, the Crown of the Empire of Fantasy was at stake.

The giant pointed to the mountain in the center of the island. At the top there was **A STONE THRONE**!

"To win the coveted crown
you must excel at climbing around.
She who can first reach the top
will take the throne, and this test will stop!"

Once more, I climbed onto the giant's shoulders to watch.

Winglet and Flamelet both grabbed on to the first rock that **stuck** out and took off. The climb to the throne had begun!

At first, Winglet was careful and quick, moving from one rock to another naturally. Flamelet moved just as fast, but after a while, they both began to slow down, getting more and more tired. The sides were steep, and they clung to the rocks.

"Winglet, hang on! Don't look down!" I yelled, hoping she could hear me.

It seemed like my positive thoughts had reached her: The princess suddenly gained ground over Flamelet, dashing **upward**!

Winglet was about to reach the Throne of the Empire!

But that's when Flamelet cried out, "Ouch! I twisted my ankle! I'm going to fall!"

Without hesitating, Winglet stopped and reached out her hand. "**HANG ON TO ME!**"

Thinking that no one was watching, Flamelet grabbed Winglet's hand — and climbed past her!

She reached the top and sat, happily, on the stone throne.

"**I won!**" she rejoiced. "I won the seventh test! The Crown of the Empire is mine!"

For all the cheese in the Kingdom of Fantasy, I couldn't let that stand! It wasn't fair!

"She can't win the crown!" I shouted to the giant. "She cheated!"

"This seat is mine," Flamelet crowed, settling comfortably on the throne. "Did I, or did I not, arrive at the top first?"

I was shaking in **ANGER**! Winglet should have won!

"So, where's the crown?" Flamelet huffed.

But the **crown** didn't appear . . .

Instead, the throne moved, as if it had come to life!

It moved, vibrated . . .

and shook Flamelet off!

Help!

# THE CROWN OF THE EMPIRE

The throne stood empty on the mountain. It was waiting for the **rightful winner!**

Cheesy creampuffs, I couldn't believe my eyes — the throne had come to life and flung Wither's daughter away! Meanwhile, Winglet had also reached the top of the mountain. She looked around, confused, as she tried to catch her breath.

What?!

"Flamelet, what are you doing on the ground?" she panted. "You won the last test. Victory is yours."

Just then, the giant looked down at Flamelet and thundered:

"You don't win this noble test.
You're a traitor, beyond the rest!
You're capable and know the kingdom well,
but are also filled with hatred and betrayal.
Smarts, balance, agility,
concentration, wisdom, responsibility:
These are all gifts of great value,
but none so much as a heart that's true!
So the crown will go to the one with finesse:
Winglet, the Rebel Princess!"

He blew the **cornet** once more, to mark the end of the seventh and final test.

Winglet, the same little Winglet who I had met when she was a baby, the daughter of beloved queen Blossom, had **passed the test**!

"I can't believe it," she murmured in shock. As soon as she sat on the throne, the most beautiful golden crown I had ever seen appeared on her lap. *Squeak!* It was the legendary . . .

# Crown of the Empire!

"Knight, we did it!" Winglet said to me, her eyes sparkling with happiness.

"You won!" I cheered.

And on the other paw, Flamelet got what she deserved! Yes, she had passed four of the tests, but she'd passed the first because of ruthlessness, the fourth because she had taken a shortcut,

and the last because she had taken advantage of Winglet's goodness!

The giant used his big stone hands to put me on the top of the mountain next to the princess. It was time to say **good-bye**.

"Thank you," I said to the giant with a deep bow. Then I turned to Winglet. "It's time to take the Crown of the Empire to Queen Blossom!"

At that moment, the throne came free from the mountain and **FLEW**, as light as a hot-air balloon!

"Wait for me, Winglet!" I exclaimed, grabbing on to the base of the throne just in time.

The giant said good-bye and explained that the throne would take us right to Crystal Castle.

*Flamelet* didn't want to be left behind. "You're not leaving without me! The crown is mine!" she yelled, trying to grab on to the throne. "You will not leave! Got that? You won't — Aaaah!"

In all the excitement, Flamelet lost her grip and fell down down down down down

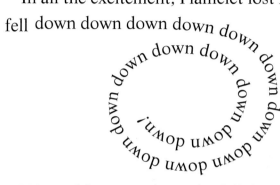

We couldn't see where she fell, but we could no longer hear her cries.

Holey cheese! Even though she was an EVIL FAIRY, I still felt sad for her. But there was nothing we could do — there was no stopping the throne.

The Island of the Seven Secrets faded into the distance as the **wind** carried us toward Crystal Castle!

# THE NEW EMPRESS

This definitely wasn't an easy journey — I was hanging on tight to the throne like stretched-out cheese, my paws dangling in the air!

"Climb up here with me, Knight!" Winglet said, helping me get more comfortable on the throne.

"Let's hope we're not too late," I said once I'd taken a seat.

What a feline fright! We darted along high in the sky, blasting through clouds. Finally, after what seemed like hours, we saw the sparkly blue spires in the distance. We had finally arrived!

Around the castle, a battle was still raging. The **invisibles** had blocked the castle! With all the dust stirred up by the fight, we couldn't tell the

Winged Defenders from their enemies.

I felt my heart jump: *Blossom* was surrounded by the Whine-Tossers, and they were about to strike her down!

The **LOYAL ARMY'S** defense hadn't worked. The Invisibles were winning!

Winglet wasn't about to give up now. "Mom, hang in there!" she called. "I'm here for you! I brought the crown!"

At that moment, the throne lit up.

The light fell over the mountains, covering Crystal Castle and the whole battlefield.

The Invisibles, who were blinded by the light, were terrified. But the light gave the **Winged Ones** their strength back! Those on the ground stood up again, and everyone looked toward the sky, amazed.

*The Rebel Princess was back!*

The throne landed next to Blossom. At first, it was hard to recognize her. The queen was pale, with her head hanging and her eyes glassed over. But slowly, thanks to the **Magic Light** coming from the throne and Winglet's presence, the queen's cheeks filled with color again.

Winglet threw her arms around her mother, crying tears of happiness.

"Here is the crown, Mom," she said, holding up the symbol of the new empire, sparkling with dazzling light.

To make the moment even more *beautiful*, Winglet got on her knees and placed the crown on the ground before Blossom. But as soon as she took her hands off the crown . . . its surface stopped shining!

Moldy mozzarella, what was going on?

Blossom lifted the crown, but it remained a simple golden crown.

Handing it back to Winglet, she said, "Try to take it in your hands again, my daughter."

Winglet did, and at her touch the crown began to sparkle like the sun again, and a sweet scent filled the air. It was the scent of strength, courage, loyalty . . . it smelled like the Rebel Princess!

Blossom's eyes shone brighter than the crown.

"Part of me has always known this day would come," she said, her voice filled with emotion. "You have brought me the crown, but I will not be the one to wear it. You have proven yourself:

*Winglet, you are the new empress!"*

Smiling, Blossom placed the Crown of the Empire of Fantasy on Winglet's head. As soon as she touched it, the crown let off the **purest light**!

Winglet was still astounded. "Mom, I don't deserve all of this!"

"But you do," said Blossom wisely. "You earned the crown, and we are all so proud of you!"

Everyone exploded in cheers.

## "Long live the empress!"

Winglet grinned, and I could tell she was feeling a million things all at once.

You are the new empress!

"Knight," Blossom said, turning to me. "You've earned my trust, as always. I knew you wouldn't let me down. You are the *best friend* I could ever ask for!"

I turned as red as the sauce on a double-cheese pizza and mumbled, "I just went along with Winglet! It was a great honor for me."

"You did much more than that," said a voice behind us.

"**Creasely!**" I cried, throwing my arms around her shell. "How did you get back?"

"Dawn and I had just beat those three rude boors when a sparkly light lit up the sky," the turtle explained. "Suddenly, here we are!"

"**Dawn!**" Winglet exclaimed, burying her face in the tiger's soft fur. "You're safe! Let's never separate again!" She looked around, her eyes sparkling. "Foxlyn, you're here, too! Narek! And . . . **LORIAN**!"

"I've returned," the dragon tamer said. "It's good to see you, Princess."

They **hugged** and said nothing more.

Lorian!

Their reunion made me melt like Swiss cheese in the sun!

Blossom smiled. "I'm so happy that you two are getting along! It was one of my greatest wishes. And, speaking of wishes, Winglet, I will tell you a secret: The Crown of the Empire will grant the person who wears it ONE WISH. But this wish must be favorable to the birth of the empire."

Winglet stood silently, thinking, but she didn't need to reflect for long. She closed her eyes, nodded, and said, "I've made my wish!"

# THE CORONATION
# CEREMONY

After the castle had been returned to its regular state, Blossom got ready for a coronation ceremony. Now that the Invisibles had been defeated, the **Harmony Stone** was back in the case. The case was closed with seven locks.

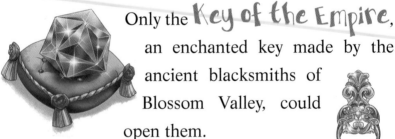

Only the **Key of the Empire**, an enchanted key made by the ancient blacksmiths of Blossom Valley, could open them.

Finally, everything was ready. Winglet could barely sit still! She took my paws. "I'm so excited. But will I ever be **GOOD ENOUGH** to take on this role?"

"Of course!" I said with a smile.

In a few days, my friend seemed to have grown up. Her eyes still had the sparkle of the Rebel Princess, but her face was much more sure. She wouldn't take off all of her necklaces and bracelets for the official crowning ceremony. The only thing she got rid of was the dragonfly clip that Flamelet had given her.

The room was packed with friends that had come with us to the island. The Winged Ones that had helped defend the castle were all there, too. Finally, **peace** had been restored!

Blossom placed the crown on Winglet's head again, and it lit up with the rays of the moon. "The Crown of the Empire is yours!" she said.

Winglet smiled and turned to the crowd. "First of all, I want to thank the heroes who joined me on my journey. Creasely: Because of your wisdom, you will be the Empire's Great Advisor! Foxlyn: You will be treasurer! And you, my dear

friend," Winglet concluded, looking at me, "will be rewarded with the title **Knight of the Empire**."

Holey cheese!

"Hooray! Well done!" the crowd cheered.

Suddenly, an icy silence fell over room. Someone new had entered: *Flamelet*!

Winglet stood up and walked to her calmly. "This is exactly what I wished for — I asked to save you. My heart tells me that our friendship wasn't completely fake, before I found out who you really were."

Flamelet hung her head. "A part of me really did care for you when I was at Crystal Castle. It was impossible not to like you. You have a big **heart**. I am very sorry."

"Everyone deserves a second chance," Winglet said. "**I forgive you!**"

Those were truly the words of a real princess —

I mean, an empress! The crown let out an even more intense light. But then . . . a **SHADOW** fell upon the room!

I forgive you!

# AN UNINVITED GUEST

It seemed as if the room had filled with thick, dark **INK**!

It seemed like the moon had been eclipsed!

It seemed like . . . Wither had entered!

She had arrived: **WITHER**, Blossom's evil twin! She whirled into the room like a tornado, yelling, "This empire will not be born!" She turned to Flamelet. "And you, my daughter! Didn't you learn anything from my example of **cruelty**? You were to bring me the crown, but instead you went over to the good side like a little fool of a fairy!" She sneered. "You disappoint me,

but now you and your friend will pay!"

Wither pointed her **WanD** at Flamelet and Winglet, ready to cast the wickedest spell . . .

But something went wrong!

A small, slimy green silhouette leaped up on Wither and attached to her face like a suction cup. It was *Mossy*!

"You will never do harm to anyone again!" the small tree frog croaked.

"Shoo, you dirty tree frog, shoo!" Wither shouted, trying to grab her, but Mossy **jUMpeD** on her head and then climbed on her arms.

Once she managed to grab Mossy, Wither pointed her wand at Winglet again. Cheese and crackers, I had to do something!

But what?

I grabbed a vase from a nearby table, and I threw myself in front of the princess, using it as a **SHIELD**!

Luckily, I didn't end up roasted by Wither's evil rays.

At that moment, the throne let out a **super-powerful** golden LIGHT that hit the witch full-on!

Noooooo!

It was the purest, most intense, and blinding glow. Those with **EVIL HEARTS** could not withstand it!

Wither covered her face and threatened, "Don't you dare bring the Empire of Fantasy back to life! I will **return**, and I will destroy it!"

Then she disappeared like a bat in the night.

I exhaled and realized I had been holding my breath the whole time. After all, I'm a bit of a 'fraidy mouse!

"Mossy!" Winglet exclaimed. "Thank you for defending me and Flamelet. Without you, the empire would have been in **SERIOUS DANGER**!"

Mossy hung her little green head. "I wanted to help you to make up for what I did! I tricked you, and I'm nothing but swamp vermin, cane mold —"

"Mossy." Winglet stopped her with a smile. "You risked your life for us. Here!"

She gave her a scroll, which the tree frog read aloud.

The Position of Great Friend

Recognition is given to this creature who has distinguished herself for having the following qualities:

courage
loyalty
kindness.

In good faith, Winglet

Mossy had tears in her eyes. "Me, a GREAT FRIEND? Really? Are you sure?"

"Completely sure!" Winglet said. "And that's not all. You will also become the Empire of Fantasy's messenger. But now, dear friends, we must continue with the party!"

# THE FIRST STEP TOWARD THE NEW EMPIRE

What followed was the most beautiful reception! There was an atmosphere of hope, and the castle buzzed with energy. It was a new era for the

**Empire of Fantasy!**

There was no telling where its borders would reach! In my heart I felt that the tasks that awaited young WINGLET, the Rebel Princess and leader of a great empire, would not be easy. But I was ready to face them at her side — especially after hearing

her *message* to all of the creatures of the new Empire of Fantasy.

Before I knew it, though, it was time to say good-bye. *Sniff* — I would miss my friends so much!

Lorian grabbed my paw and shook it firmly. "Narek will take you home. I hope to see you soon, Knight!"

I smiled at him. "Take care of Winglet!"

Lorian nodded and put his hand on the fairy's shoulder. Those two had **finally** learned to get along!

Then the princess turned

You are a true empress!

to me. "Knight, if there is anything that I have learned on this journey, it's that sometimes nothing is as it seems. Traitors can turn out to be friends, and a **heart** of gold can hide within an **ENEMY**."

"You're right!" I said. "But sometimes everything is exactly as it seems: like you. You seem like a true empress — and you are!"

Purr, purr, purr!

Suddenly, a big, soft, and powerful paw pushed my back. I turned and came snout-to-snout with **Dawn**!

The tiger closed her eyes and let out a deep rumble!

"Dawn agrees with you, and she

is **PURRING** to say good-bye!" Winglet giggled.

I smiled and gave the big tiger a little scratch under the chin. Now that I had gotten to know her, she didn't scare me . . . much!

I hugged **Foxlyn** (who had finally stopped asking for loans!), and then it was time to say good-bye to **Creasely**.

"It has really been an unforgettable adventure. I will miss you a lot!" I said, kissing her foot.

My tortoise friend looked me square in the eye and said, "I will miss you, too, brave Knight."

Blossom said good-bye as I climbed up onto the

I will miss you a lot!

Emerald Dragon. "Dear Knight, as always, your **courage** and your NOBLE spirit have helped to save our kingdom! It's nice to know that we can count on you!" She gave me a warm hug.

We took flight just as the light of dawn began to spill across the sky.

My journey might be coming to an end, but the **Empire of Fantasy** was beginning its new life with Winglet, the Rebel Empress!

# A SURPRISE FOR BENJAMIN

The big day had arrived — *Fantastical Stories* was **being released**!

Early in the morning, before going to *The Rodent's Gazette,* I took my nephew Benjamin to get his copy of the book. I couldn't wait see his face when he saw the **SURPRISE** I had for him!

As we walked to the bookstore down the street, a smile stretched across his snout. "Uncle, I love stories about **fantastical worlds**! I can't wait to read them."

"I really hope that you'll love the book. I put my whole heart into it!" I told him, wrapping him in a big hug.

When we arrived, there was a long line in front of the bookseller. The new book already looked like it would be a huge success!

When we reached the front of the line, Benjamin proudly asked for his copy of Fantastical Stories. When he held it in his paws, he was shocked. "Uncle G! The pictures POP OUt of the book!"

"I thought that, this time, I wouldn't just write a novel about my trip on the wings of fantasy," I said. "I wanted to think of a different kind of book: a POP-UP book of the Kingdom of Fantasy!"

Benjamin was wide-eyed looking at all the creatures and landscapes that magically opened up before him.

"Ooooooh!" he squeaked when the Emerald Dragon unfolded his powerful paper wings.

"Ahhhhh!" he cried, looking at Monsieur Arach pop out suddenly.

He was quiet when he saw the big rock giant.

I, on the other paw, will admit that I got a little teary when I saw the figures of Creasely, Foxlyn, Mossy, Dawn, Lorian, and Winglet appear on the pages.

They were my **friends**, and they were right there on the pages of a book that made them seem so alive and so close. Thanks to this book, my adventure will live forever — a tail-twistingly good adventure, or my name isn't

Stilton, Geronimo Stilton!

Don't miss any of my adventures in the Kingdom of Fantasy!

## THE KINGDOM OF FANTASY

## THE QUEST FOR PARADISE:
THE RETURN TO THE KINGDOM OF FANTASY

## THE AMAZING VOYAGE:
THE THIRD ADVENTURE IN THE KINGDOM OF FANTASY

## THE DRAGON PROPHECY:
THE FOURTH ADVENTURE IN THE KINGDOM OF FANTASY

## THE VOLCANO OF FIRE:
THE FIFTH ADVENTURE IN THE KINGDOM OF FANTASY

## THE SEARCH FOR TREASURE:
THE SIXTH ADVENTURE IN THE KINGDOM OF FANTASY

## THE ENCHANTED CHARMS:
THE SEVENTH ADVENTURE IN THE KINGDOM OF FANTASY

## THE PHOENIX OF DESTINY:
AN EPIC KINGDOM OF FANTASY ADVENTURE

## THE HOUR OF MAGIC:
THE EIGHTH ADVENTURE IN THE KINGDOM OF FANTASY

## THE WIZARD'S WAND:
THE NINTH ADVENTURE IN THE KINGDOM OF FANTASY

## THE SHIP OF SECRETS:
THE TENTH ADVENTURE IN THE KINGDOM OF FANTASY

## THE DRAGON OF FORTUNE:
AN EPIC KINGDOM OF FANTASY ADVENTURE

## THE GUARDIAN OF THE REALM:
THE ELEVENTH ADVENTURE IN THE KINGDOM OF FANTASY

## THE ISLAND OF DRAGONS:
THE TWELFTH ADVENTURE IN THE KINGDOM OF FANTASY

## THE BATTLE FOR THE CRYSTAL CASTLE:
THE THIRTEENTH ADVENTURE IN THE KINGDOM OF FANTASY

# Don't miss a single fabumouse adventure!

## Up Next:

# ABOUT THE AUTHOR

Born in New Mouse City, Mouse Island, **GERONIMO STILTON** is Rattus Emeritus of Mousomorphic Literature and of Neo-Ratonic Comparative Philosophy. For the past twenty years, he has been running *The Rodent's Gazette*, New Mouse City's most widely read daily newspaper.

Stilton was awarded the Ratitzer Prize for his scoops on *The Curse of the Cheese Pyramid* and *The Search for Sunken Treasure*. He has also received the Andersen 2000 Prize for Personality of the Year. One of his bestsellers won the 2002 eBook Award for world's best ratling's electronic book. His works have been published all over the globe.

In his spare time, Mr. Stilton collects antique cheese rinds and plays golf. But what he most enjoys is telling stories to his nephew Benjamin.